things
that
are

ANDREW CLEMENTS

things

that

are

PHILOMEL BOOKS

PATRICIA LEE GAUCH, EDITOR

PHILOMEL BOOKS
A division of Penguin Young Readers Group.
Published by The Penguin Group.
Penguin Group (USA) Inc., 375 Hudson Street, New York, NY 10014, U.S.A.
Penguin Group (Canada), 90 Eglinton Avenue East, Suite 700, Toronto, Ontario
M4P 2Y3, Canada (a division of Pearson Penguin Canada Inc.).
Penguin Books Ltd, 80 Strand, London WC2R 0RL, England.
Penguin Ireland, 25 St. Stephen's Green, Dublin 2, Ireland (a division
of Penguin Books Ltd).
Penguin Group (Australia), 250 Camberwell Road, Camberwell, Victoria 3124,
Australia (a division of Pearson Australia Group Pty Ltd).
Penguin Books India Pvt Ltd, 11 Community Centre, Panchsheel Park,
New Delhi - 110 017, India.
Penguin Group (NZ), 67 Apollo Drive, Rosedale, North Shore 0632,
New Zealand (a division of Pearson New Zealand Ltd).
Penguin Books (South Africa) (Pty) Ltd, 24 Sturdee Avenue, Rosebank,
Johannesburg 2196, South Africa.
Penguin Books Ltd, Registered Offices: 80 Strand, London WC2R 0RL, England.

Published simultaneously in Canada.   Printed in the United States of America.
Design by Semadar Megged.   Text set in 11-point Trump Mediaeval.
Library of Congress Cataloging-in-Publication Data is available upon request.
ISBN 978-0-399-24691-3
13 15 17 19 20 18 16 14 12

Again, for Rebecca

vibrations

The phone vibrates under my pillow—*dash; dot, dot, dot*. That's B. For "Bobby." The second call from him on the same night. Which is good news. Very good news. Even at two in the morning. Because our earlier conversation didn't go as far as I wanted it to. I need to say something else to him. Something important.

Dash; dot, dot, dot—

I push the answer button and I use my warmest voice, sweet and sleepy. "Hey—hi."

Nothing.

I press the phone against my ear and talk louder. "Bobby? Bobby? It's Alicia."

Faint voices, one of them his. Plus a lot of hiss and static.

And right away I know what this is. It's not another call from Bobby. It's a mistake. He has one of those candy-bar cell phones, and he keeps it in his pocket. And when he sat down or bent over, something pushed against the redial button. By mistake. So now I'm eaves-dropping on a conversation in New York City, eight hundred miles away.

It's a guy talking, someone I don't know, and his voice sounds odd. I stifle a yawn and try to focus on the words.

". . . and that is precisely what you do not under-stand. There are other forces at work. And all this anger is unproductive—especially since you and I have com-mon interests. I was hoping—"

Bobby interrupts.

"We don't have *anything* in common, not one thing."

"I am deeply disappointed that you seem so unwill-ing to help me. Because I'm sure you can. And I really must *insist*. One way or another, you *are* going to help me."

"What's that supposed to mean?" Bobby's voice is hard and flat.

"It means that, like it or not, we are linked now. And because . . ."

Harsh hissing noises and random phone button tones. Then silence.

And my phone gives a little shake that means "call ended."

I'm tempted to call Bobby back, make sure he's all right.

But I don't want him to think I'm worried about him. Even if I am.

And I don't want our next conversation to begin by accident.

And really, what I have to tell him? I don't want to talk about it on the phone. We need to be in the same room. No static, no hum, no distance. Close. Breathing the same air.

So I tuck the phone back under my pillow, pull the quilt up over my shoulders, and yawn, and I shut my eyes, and I let it all go. For now.

Because everything will have to wait until tomorrow. Until morning. Until Thursday.

chapter 2

moonless

I swat the clock and it stops buzzing. I blink my eyes to scatter the last of my dreams, a scary one about Bobby and this angry man who keeps shouting, "Fee, fie, foe, fum!"

And I sit up, take a look around, and then shut my eyes and flop back into my pillow.

Yes. I'm Alicia. It's me. Here in bed.

And right away a docudrama about life on earth flashes onto the small screen inside my head. With me in the starring role.

Me.

Four and a half years ago, *me* wasn't much of a word. I was an eighth-grader then—kind of popular, kind of pretty, kind of interesting, kind of smart, kind of aimless and friendly and snotty and carefree and anxious and shallow and deep and wistful and perky and moody and . . . kind of ordinary. An ordinary me on an ordinary path to an ordinary high-school-and-college-and-grad-school-and-career-and-home-and-family-and-second-career-and-retirement kind of a life.

All of which sounds kind of heavenly right now.

Because halfway through eighth grade I banged my head, and something stopped working, something neural and retinal, something that affected both my eyes. And since that moment I've been blind.

No one could figure it out, at least not in any practical, fixable way. So I've been learning to cope.

I've had help, of course. My parents have been great, first fighting for the best specialists, the best care, the best analysis. Then fighting for the best teaching, the best equipment, the best of everything. Hard times for them. Especially Mom. Or maybe she just lets more worry seep out into the air than Daddy does.

The people at the Hadley School for the Blind have been great too—kind and very patient.

It was dark back then. I wore a brave face for my mom and dad, but so much had disappeared. And after a year or two I was headed that way myself, feeling more and more lost.

And then Bobby happened.

Bobby.

He's been away almost three weeks now. I can't help thinking about him, and I loved talking to him last night. Except I wanted to say so much more.

He won't be back from his auditions in New York until Sunday, three more days. He's hoping to get accepted at a music school, hoping to start this fall, studying trumpet, jazz and classical. And all his college choices are far away from Chicago. Far away from me.

Before I met Bobby, I had lost most of my hopes, my plans, my dreams. I had lost my view of the future. The blindness had its hooks in deep.

What changed me most wasn't just our friendship. Which is turning into something more. Maybe.

What changed me was being able to help someone. I know that if I hadn't helped Bobby two years ago, he wouldn't have found his way back from his own temporary disability, his own brand of blindness. Helping him made me see I could do more to help myself.

And about two years ago I reenrolled in high school. Not school for the blind. High school. That was a few months after I met Bobby. The timing wasn't a coincidence. The things he and I went through back then changed me.

Because a moment came when I had to choose whether I was going to be blind or not, and I chose. And now I'm not blind. I still can't see, but I'm not blind. And I keep making that choice. Every day.

And what's happened to me during the two years since Bobby burst into my life?

Now I am a better thinker, a better reader, a better writer—at least I think I am. I even play guitar—badly, but I'm learning. And now I can type like crazy, about eighty words a minute. And I read Braille faster than most of my teachers. I've got a portable Braille keyboard, and I can fly through novels, textbooks, web pages, reference books, anything on a screen. I plug the thing into my laptop and it translates the output, pushing up pins to form the symbols. I touch, I feel, I read, I see. And soon I'm getting an audible GPS hookup—uses a Bluetooth connection and uplinks to satellites, eyes in the sky. And the new electronic voices and the new screen readers are fantastic, and I'm staying on top of all that stuff. Because in the land of the blind, it's geekness or weakness. I am the techno queen.

And I've used my new sensitivities, used the strange freedoms my blindness has given me. Freedom from distractions. Freedom to be alone. Freedom from cliques and gossip and comparisons—all the junk that can make school feel like a snake pit. I've used my freedom to crunch through three years of high school in two. And I got great SAT scores, and my class rank is up in the top three percent.

This isn't bragging. And I'm not doing all this to make my parents proud, or to show the world how a blind girl is as capable as the next kid.

So why am I pushing myself?

Bobby.

He's going to college this fall, and so am I. I'm going too. Because I am *not* going to be left behind. I am not going to be the girl back home, back in his past life. I'm no musician, so I know we won't be at the same school. But I can be somewhere near, somewhere in his life. In the present. Maybe.

Another maybe.

And maybe all this Bobby stuff is a dream. Which is why we have to talk, just the two of us. Soon.

Because I know how cruel dreams can be.

Every night in my dreams I see perfectly for hours and hours—maple trees, streams and mountains, the city skyline, the faces I love, tulips and sunsets. All those stored-up images.

And the moon. In my dreams I always see the moon, bright against the sky.

And every morning I learn I'm blind all over again. That's the cruel part. I open my eyes and stare: darkness, but not the night sky. It's a wall, dull and blackish brown, and very near. No sun, no stars, no moon.

Makes it hard to get out of bed. Like today, right now.

Gertie's here, and that's good. She's a German shepherd, and I can hear her stir and stretch and yawn in her doggie bed across the room. I got her almost six months ago. I'd become good enough at tapping my white cane that my counselor decided I could use a guide dog. A new level of moonless independence.

And really, Gertie's wonderful, like a low-tech organ transplant, a set of eyes walking alongside, complete with an extra brain.

My turn to stretch and yawn. I didn't rest well last night. Two phone calls from Bobby—one on purpose, and one that scared me. An argument . . . right? It's fuzzy. Along with a bunch of other things in my life.

It feels like there's so much at risk right now.

Which is why I have to get up and face the world, deal with it, be positive, make progress.

That's what I tell myself.

But I don't move.

Gertie jumps onto the bed and nudges me with her nose. She's always direct, always definite. And now she needs to go out. I almost push her away, send her off to find Mom. But Gertie is my responsibility, my eyes.

Besides, Mom and Dad aren't here. Thursday is my morning to sleep late. Both my parents are on campus by now, one teaching and the other being taught. We live practically in the middle of the University of Chicago, so even when they're gone, they're close.

They're always close, especially Mom. If she could crawl inside my skin with me, if she could be blind along with me, or instead of me, she would.

I'm glad she's studying again, getting her Ph.D. in Elizabethan poetry. She used to do a lot of writing for a group of marketing consultants, a job she didn't like much, and my blindness gave her a reason to quit. Which let her focus on helping me—even when I wanted to do more and more on my own. So now the degree program keeps her busy, which makes both of us a little less crazy. I mean, I know my blindness has been tough for her. The truth? I've made the adjustment better than she has. Which is one of the reasons I love Thursday morning so much: I get to wake up when I want, pick out the clothes I want to wear, eat whatever I want for breakfast, and wander over to the university library when I'm good and ready. All on my own—no advice, no directions, no silent frowns. And no timekeeper. Unless you count Gertie.

I'm enrolled in regular high school, but I don't attend on a regular schedule. Thanks to the Individuals with Disabilities Education Act, I get to do flextime and individualized study projects.

So I use my special status under the law. I work the system. And today I'm legally truant, sleeping in.

Another nudge.

"Okay, Gertie. It's all right. Good girl."

I'm up, and I pull on my robe and find a slipper, and I've got the other one, and now that I'm on the move, Gertie jumps off the bed and goes into guide-dog mode, even though she's not wearing her harness. She's completely unselfish, so focused on my needs, always so close—like I'm the president and she's my Secret Service agent.

Would Gertie take a bullet for me? Absolutely.

But here at home I don't need much help, so I release her, and I hear her trot ahead to the end of the hallway, hear her claws click down the back stairs to the kitchen door that opens into the fenced backyard. I follow, much more slowly.

When I get to the back door, first I reach up and to the right. I push the alarm status button, and a strong male voice announces, "System is armed." So I find the keypad, push the four-digit code, and the same voice says, "System is disarmed."

My parents never leave me at home without turning on the alarm system. I'm their baby, and the alarm system is the babysitter. One of the babysitters.

I open the door.

There's a walnut tree in the center of the backyard, home to a pair of squirrels. One of the few times Gertie gets to be purely a dog is when she blasts out the door in the morning and streaks toward that tree, trying to catch a warm meal. And today, like every day, after the scramble I hear the squirrels, twenty feet up, scolding my dog.

Classic scene.

Except I have to imagine it, make my own pictures.

I barely think anymore about the way I see without eyesight.

But at a moment like this, with cold February air in my face, when I become aware of the process, I'm still amazed at how well it works. Because my four good senses pick up all this information, and that data sprays a stream of words across my mind, and those words create images—my own private movie. Which may or may not be physically accurate. And that's fine with me. I'm not afraid of ambiguity. I use my words and I see what I want to see, what I need to see.

And I love my words and I'm so glad it all works. Otherwise, this morning scene would be nothing but vibrations on my eardrums—invisible dog chasing invisible squirrels.

Invisible.

I got so angry at Bobby when I first met him. He told me he was invisible. I thought he was mocking me. Because I'd been struggling with that word. And that feeling. Invisible.

Because blindness tries to make everything disappear—friends, family, life, self.

But Bobby wasn't mocking me. He wasn't being metaphorical. Or metaphysical. All that came later.

That first day when he told me he was invisible, he meant it. He was talking physics—cold, hard physics: He'd woken up one morning and his body had stopped reflecting light. For real. It was science, an actual phenomenon. He had just happened to be at the right place at the right moment when the right conditions converged. Or maybe I should call them the *wrong* conditions. Either way, this precise set of interacting circumstances had created an observable effect. On Bobby, on his physical body.

And two years ago he and I were the ones who finally figured things out, figured out how he could get back to normal—as normal as anyone can be after an experience like that.

I mean, it's not like Bobby and I figured it out entirely on our own. We had some big-time help thinking about the problem. Both our dads are completely into physics—real scientists. Supergeeks. Mine looks at outer space—he teaches astrophysics at the University of Chicago. And Bobby's dad looks at inner space—hunting for particles, and the parts of the parts of the parts of the particles. He works with the Tevatron team at FermiLab, which is in Batavia, Illinois, about an hour west of here.

The two dads squished their brains all over the invisibility problem, trying to understand the physics, trying to see how to reverse the process. But in the end, they were stumped.

And me, the blind girl? I was the one who actually made the connection that helped Bobby readjust his body. And I also helped him find some courage. Because stepping into the unknown is always a risk.

So, yes, the blind girl saved the day. In my docudrama of life on earth.

But I didn't use physics. Or math. Or spectroscopic analysis.

I used intuition. I used insight. I used my words.

Because, honestly, physics is not my friend. At all.

In fact, I practically hate physics, always have—even though I can talk the talk and grasp the concepts. But I won't give my heart to a subject that can be so harsh, so unforgiving.

Maybe just to bother my dad.

He would never admit it, but he was hoping for a child who would carry his own brilliance into the future.

Didn't happen.

And four years ago my dislike of the p-word intensified. Because optics is a branch of physics, right? If physical laws were truly my friend, I wouldn't have become blind. Or stayed that way.

And then there's the Bobby phenomenon. Because what turned him invisible that morning two years ago? My not-friend again, physics. And the problems caused by that episode are not over.

On the other hand, if the physics hadn't zapped him, would Bobby have bumped into me at the U of C library that day? Would we have become . . . friends? No, probably not.

But we could have met some other way. Because what if . . .

What if.

I hate what-ifs almost as much as I hate physics.

Which is logical, in an ironic sort of way. Because the study of physics is all about asking, "What if . . . ?"

So I guess I hate logic this morning. And irony.

But I love sarcasm. Except I sort of hate that I love it.

Sort of the way that I hate how Bobby and I have become such good *pals*. Which is a sarcastic comment.

So many things to hate.

And love.

Like secrets. I love keeping secrets. Because I love to be trusted.

Bobby trusted me with his secret. About the invisibility. That single act of trust started to pull me out of my darkness.

We kept the invisibility a secret. And now, two years later, it's still a secret. And with good reason.

Bobby didn't want to tell me about it. He didn't want to tell anyone about the invisibility. He was afraid of being turned into a freak show, afraid of having his life taken over by some agency, afraid of being poked and probed and analyzed, afraid of the physicists and the biologists and the geneticists, afraid of the spies, afraid of governments everywhere.

We had to face an ugly fact: There are people in this world who would actually kill to find out how to make living flesh and blood disappear and reappear at will. Because every intelligence agency, every military planner, every dictator, every terrorist group, every unstable whacko in the world would love to know how to make a human being drop out of sight. It's a dangerous technology, the kind that can shift the balance of power and shake nations. And in the wrong hands, it would have a terrible impact.

Because launching a fleet of invisible agents would be like making everyone else blind—to their presence, their movements, their activities. As if public safety or nuclear security or even a simple airplane trip isn't already scary enough. As if nations don't have a hard enough time making peace with the enemies they can actually *see*.

And that's why everyone who knows what happened to Bobby has to keep it a secret. Even now. Especially now.

And here's another secret: I want Bobby to come home. To me. I don't want him in New York City for one more second. Because this girl he's met there, Gwen? I know she's wonderful. And strong.

And something happened there in New York, something that made Bobby tell Gwen about the secret. The invisibility.

Which used to be *our* secret, his and mine.

For the past two years Bobby has thought of me as his girlfriend. Which is not a secret.

But it hasn't been completely true.

"My girlfriend, Alicia"—that's just been a thing Bobby could say, a convenience, a way he could avoid the pressures and the messiness of having a real girlfriend, a full-hearted relationship. "My girlfriend, Alicia" has also been how he's avoided the feeling that he should be *looking* for a girlfriend. Because he's basically a solitary person—something we have in common. And being able to say that has made him feel connected, sort of settled, I think.

And we have felt connected. We have.

But I haven't been his girlfriend. I've been his friend who is a girl.

Still, we're close. And if we can just get some time to talk . . . Even these past three weeks when Bobby's been in New York, even after meeting Gwen, the girl with the golden violin, the girl with poetry in her fingertips, I don't think any of that has shaken our closeness. I'm sure of that. Even as he's turning away and thinking ahead, even as he's heading off for college, Bobby and I have a strong connection, something that could be even more real.

That's what my heart tells me.

It feels like I'm thinking mostly of me. I can't help it. I do think of me. Because things that affect Bobby affect me. They bump against my heart.

And this girl Gwen? She's probably beautiful. Because anyone who can play the violin like she does has to be pretty, or at least seem pretty.

And I ought to slap myself for being so shallow, for being worried about what some other girl *looks* like. I mean, I've been blind for four years. I barely know what *I* look like anymore.

And Bobby? I've never seen his face, not with my eyes.

But his voice, the tone of his thoughts, the things he finds funny and the way he laughs, the way he sometimes slips his hand into mine, the way he leans against me when we walk, the little tunes he hums—these are things I have heard and felt and known. These are things I love.

Which makes me sound like I've got a silly crush.

It's more than that, I know it is. And that makes me scared.

But it's not the new girl in Manhattan who scares me. It's not Bobby and me graduating from high school. It's not him going east to college and me going who-knows-where. And it's not my blindness. None of that stuff scares me. Because I can adjust for those things. I can address those things because I can *see* them.

It's the things I can't see. Especially the invisibility business.

It's stirring up again, I know it is. Why else would Bobby's father keep dropping by? He's come to our house a lot in the past two months, and each time my father and he have spent hours and hours out back in my dad's study. Dr. Phillips and my dad haven't spent that kind of time together for almost two years.

And why did Mom and Dad go suddenly silent when I came into the kitchen for dinner yesterday?

And when Bobby and I talked last night, why was he so vague about what happened in New York, about why he had to tell Gwen about the invisibility?

I hate vagueness.

And that argument Bobby was having, that conversation I heard by mistake in the middle of my dreams last night—what was that about?

It's like there's this constant hum, these whispers I can't quite hear. And I can feel these new people, these obscure threats lurking at the edges of my life, pushing in at me. And at Bobby.

These are the things that scare me.

And I can't shake this feeling that everything's at risk.

Which is why I get so desperate for something to hold on to, something comforting, something true, something beautiful. Or someone. Like Bobby.

Beauty is truth, truth beauty.

John Keats wrote that, and he got it right.

But truth is also a stone-cold killer. It kills the lies. All of them. Dead.

And my beauty, my love, my future, my dreams? How many of them will turn out to be lies?

"Sooner or later, reality occurs."

That's a quote from Uncle Arthur, a friend of the family, a kind old banker, a man who loved his wife and his children and his twin brother and his yacht. And during his long life he saw a lot of people try to juggle numbers and use phony accounting to avoid the truth.

I'm not going to do that. I'm facing facts, facing reality. My reality, *my* life.

Like the blindness. For me, it's just the way things are.

Things are.

Are.

Makes me sound like a pirate: *Arrrr.*

That's me, the pirate girl, black patches on both eyes.

But I'm dealing with it.

Because I'm not wishing or hoping or dreaming. About anything.

I'm facing things as they are.

"Gertie—here."

One short command, and she obeys instantly. Such an intelligent creature. And so loving.

I pat her, and I hug her, and I give her way more

affection than I'm supposed to. Because Gertie's a work-ing dog, not a pet.

But she needs love. We both need love.

There's some truth. And some beauty too.

So it's a Thursday, and I need to eat breakfast and take a shower and let Gertie guide me to the library.

Because I need to make some progress today, keep figuring out what life is like for me. Keep trying to see if Bobby is still part of that life.

And as I go to the cupboard and sniff out the cinna-mon bread for my toast, I wonder if it's one of those mornings when the moon is visible.

Because I love that, catching a glimpse of the moon during the day, hiding in the pale winter sky.

And there it is. I see it perfectly.

chapter 3
voices

I step slowly down the stairs from my front porch.

One, two, three, four, five.

I don't walk down. I step. Until I get my bearings, I step as if each footfall might be my last, as if I were walking along the edge of a cliff in the dark. Because being blind can feel like that, if you let it.

But once I'm through the gate and on the sidewalk, I turn left and I walk with purpose, left hand on Gertie's harness handle, right hand on the brown leather bag that hangs from my shoulder.

And to the casual observer, I'm sure I look confident enough, even self-assured. But every step is an exercise in faith. And that's okay. I think that's true for everyone. Being blind just makes the need for faith more obvious.

And now I'm turning onto Fifty-fifth Street in Hyde Park, just north of the University of Chicago campus. I'm on my way to the library.

Walking a familiar route like this always puts my

mind in this quiet, listening state. I get some of my best ideas for writing on my way to the library.

And sometimes when I'm at the library sitting in my study room, I can feel the books all around me, millions of them. And I picture myself walking among the stacks, and I choose a shelf, any shelf, and I walk along and let one hand bump along the spines. All those silent books. They keep their backs toward me. I stop and pull one from its place, feel the texture of the cover, and I open the book and smell that rich, deep scent of paper and ink and time. And if the book is old enough, and the paper is thick enough, and the letterpress pushed hard enough, I can drift a fingertip across a page and feel the tiny impressions, feel the words resting there. All those silent pages. At the library.

And that tempts me to complain.

But I don't let myself think about all those silent books I can never see.

I think about the thousands of books in Braille. And thousands more in audio—more books than I'll ever have time to touch or hear, not if I live three lifetimes.

So I don't complain as I step along the inky sidewalks of Chicago, and I remember why I always love the library, no matter what. So many good reasons.

First of all, the library is out. And out is important to me.

Second, the library is so alive—all that reading and thinking.

Then there's the law: If I'm not attending my regular high school in the regular way, I have to give my advisor evidence that I've been doing school-like activities at school-like places. Like a library. And keeping my teachers happy is important to me.

This library is also where I met Bobby, where we had our first conversations, our first arguments.

And Bobby is . . . well, important to me.

And brushing past his name, I feel my heart expand, feel my throat tighten.

But I snap into real time as a gust of wind hits me full in the face, cold and gritty, and I catch a faint whiff of Lake Michigan. Which means I'm facing east. Probably.

Gertie feels the sudden hesitation in my step and freezes, yanks me to a full stop. And as if it was my idea, I say, "Gertie—wait. Good girl."

I still feel the wind, and I think I still smell the lake. So that's a puzzle.

Because I ought to be facing south now, ought to be able to feel the sun on my face at this time of day. Unless it's too cloudy. Which it is. Probably.

So that means I've gotten turned around. Probably.

I hate feeling lost.

Home to the university library is a seven-block, eighteen-minute obstacle course with excellent curb cuts and dependable ice and snow removal, and I've walked it hundreds of times with my white cane, and dozens of times more recently with Gertie.

Doesn't matter. It's still easy to get muddled, to lose my step count, to lose sight of my mental map. Especially if I start thinking about Bobby.

Being lost is a lot better now that Gertie's with me. At least we're lost together. I have to keep reminding myself that the dog has absolutely no idea where we are or where we're going. She'll make sure I don't walk into a tree or drop into a pothole or get crushed by a taxi. But staying on course is my job.

I pull off my right glove and touch the watch on my left wrist. It vibrates to tell me hours and minutes. It's eleven thirty-seven. Which means that the carillon at Rockefeller Chapel will chime in twenty-three minutes. And when I hear those bells ring out above the city sounds, I'll know where I am again.

But I can't stand still that long. For one thing, it's too cold. For another, I don't have that kind of patience right now, and neither does Gertie. She hates standing still.

So here on this corner that could be Fifty-fifth and Woodlawn, or Fifty-sixth and Greenwood, or Fifty-seventh and Ingleside, I need to ask for help.

Which isn't quite true. I never actually have to ask. I just need to change my face.

The face I'm wearing now says, "I'm fine, and I know where I am and where I'm going, and I don't need your pity or your help, so don't mess with me or my dog." It's a semi-tough, semi-self-sufficient sort of a face, my alone-in-the-city face.

And standing here with Gertie, feeling her shift her

weight from paw to paw, eager to get moving, I realize something: When I'm out walking with Bobby, I don't think about my face at all; I think about his. And again, my heart sighs.

But now I need to put on my lost face: a slight frown, eyebrows bunched together, right hand up near my face with two fingers touching my chin, a trace of uncertainty in the way I stand, in the tilt of my head.

And I start a slow count: one, two, three, four, five . . .

"Need any help?"

Five seconds—rarely takes more than ten.

It's a guy, young, sounds nice. Probably a college kid.

I smile toward the voice. "Thanks. I'm a little turned around. I'm going to the Regenstein Library on Fifty-seventh, between Ellis and University."

"Well, this is Fifty-sixth and Ellis, and you're aimed south toward Fifty-seventh Street, so you're not far. I'm going right past there. Want to walk together?"

"No, that's all right."

"Really, it's not a problem."

"No, I'll be fine. Thanks again."

The truth is I'd rather be alone with my own thoughts. Because I can't walk with a complete stranger in silence. I can spend hours in silence with my friend Nancy, because Nancy gets it, she understands me. She always has. She's one of the only close friends I still have from back in eighth grade, back before the blindness.

And I can spend time being quiet with my dad too. And with Bobby.

But with a stranger, there would have to be small talk. I'm no good at small talk. Which is another reason I like the library so much: I can be with other people, but I don't have to talk to them. Which qualifies me as truly antisocial. And there it is again: things as they are.

Alicia! One quick question, if you don't mind.

You again? I forgot you were here.

I'm always here, Sister.

Sad, but true. Your question?

Don't you think the kid was just trying to be nice! And aren't you getting a little too comfortable being alone with your little heart-dreams! I mean, what if you were supposed to meet that boy today! What if that guy you just brushed off was destined to become your new best friend, the one person who stays close, who stays true, who cares about you your whole life!

First of all, Miss Nosey Brain, that was four questions, not one. And second, butt out, okay? Besides, I don't believe in destiny. Not today, not ever. What is, is; what happens, happens. Period.

Okay, okay, no need to snarl. Just thought I'd ask. But I'll keep watching your little drama. With deep interest.

So kind of you.

Don't I know it, Sister.

And stop calling me Sister.

You're in charge. Sister.

That bossy little voice in my head has been speaking up a lot in the past few weeks. Very annoying.

But I'm glad she doesn't let me kid myself. And she's so persistent. And observant.

I mean, maybe I *should* believe in destiny today. Because maybe Bobby's never coming back to me. Maybe that dream is over. Or maybe it's dying a long, slow death.

But my heart pushes that thought away.

Still, I make a mental note: Be more friendly next time you get lost.

Because I know there'll be a next time.

Six more minutes of walking, and I'm in the broad courtyard of the library, and I'm thinking ahead, because swinging doors plus lots of pedestrian traffic plus a dog on a harness are a challenge. And I know I've got about thirty steps to go when Gertie jerks me to a sudden stop. Again.

"Hey, *great* dog! Purebred shepherd, right? What a beauty—can I pet him?"

Terrific. An uninvited dog lover, butting into my life, breaking my concentration. Happens about once a week.

Which makes me want to say, "Would you ever suddenly grab the steering wheel of a car someone else was driving? Or would you reach over with your foot and stomp on the brake just because you felt like it? Because that's pretty much what you're doing right now."

But I don't say that.

I smile politely, as if he's the first person who's ever asked me that question, and I say, "Actually, you shouldn't pet her. She's working now."

"So it's a girl, huh? Doesn't look like she's working. She's just standing here. Hey, can I give her some pretzels?"

As he talks, I hear the location of his voice change, dropping closer to the ground, probably squatting down in front of the dog. And I'm surprised Gertie's being so tolerant, which isn't like her. She usually tries to pull me right past an intruding admirer.

And I can picture this guy. He's got a sophomore voice, and he's trying to make it sound extra deep and mature, and he's pouring his biggest smile into it. Kind of cocky, probably thinks he's heaven's gift to girls. Maybe nineteen, maybe a white baseball cap on his head, backpack on his back, a Vonnegut novel sticking out of his coat pocket, thinks he knows everything because he's smart enough to be at the U of C. And he thinks he's going to score points with the blind girl by being nice to her puppy dog.

Or . . . he could be a really nice guy who's never seen a real live guide dog before. Dense, but nice.

No—I don't think so. This one's an idiot.

Time to move on.

"Look, don't mess with my dog, okay? And do some outside reading on guide dogs and blind people and basic courtesy when you get a minute, all right? Now get out of the way."

I pull Gertie to the left and march, my jaw clenched, half hoping that we knock this guy flat on his back. And if he wants to make something of it, fine, because me and Gertie, we've got him outnumbered.

"*Sheesh!*" he says. "Not very *nice* . . . Alicia."

My name. And a different voice when he says it.

I stop in my tracks and whip around to face him. "You *rat* . . . you are the *worst* . . ."

Because now he's laughing. Bobby's laughing at me.

Which is not the way I pictured his homecoming. Not at all.

chapter 4
friend

Bobby and I are inside the library, walking toward the elevators.

I don't know why I feel like I need to hold myself back a little, hide how glad I am to see him. But I do.

So . . . want to hear why you're holding back?

As if you would know what I'm feeling.

Didn't you have your heart set on a tender, private moment, when your precious Bobby finally got back from New York? And . . . it didn't happen. Too bad, huh?

Not at all. In case you didn't notice, we met right out in front of the library, people all around us—hardly the place for a . . . a display of affection. We had a nice hug. It was very . . . sweet.

Except it wasn't really what you were hoping for, right? I mean, you're being cheerful about it, but you can't fool me. And aren't you just dying to know how Bobby really feels about the talented and sensitive Gwen, the girl with the golden violin? It has to be completely on your mind . . . am I right? And you're feeling vulnerable, don't want to be wounded. Again.

Just shut up, okay? And stop sounding all superior. You don't know everything, not by a long shot.

But I'm right about this one, Tootsie.

Stop calling me Tootsie.

Sure thing. Tootsie.

I shut off the head chatter, and to prove I'm *not* vulnerable, I say, "I'm really glad you're back."

He slips his hand into mine, and says, "Me too."

Long, cool fingers. And a heart flutter. I can't help it.

I manage to say, "So how come you didn't say you were coming home when you called last night?"

He laughs. "What, and miss a chance to surprise you? How'd you like my Joe College act out there? Pretty good, right?"

"Pretty mean. You're just *mean*, Bobby Phillips. Mean." But he knows I'm not mad about that. We've been playing this game for more than a year, where he puts on a phony voice and tries to hook me into a conversation. He's got skills, and I'm blind—a perfect setup for an amateur impressionist.

I say, "I thought your last college visit wasn't till Saturday."

He drops my hand, and I hear him push the elevator button.

And he doesn't take my hand again. Couldn't he have pushed the button with his other hand? Did he *want* to let go of my hand?

Overanalyzing. You're overanalyzing, Tootsie.

He says, "Yeah, but I got the audition moved up to yesterday. And then I went to the airport at five o'clock this morning, flew standby, got home at eight-thirty, and here I am."

The elevator doors open, and Gertie hesitates. She doesn't like small rooms with funny doors and floors that shake. But the three of us are in, the doors close, and we're going up.

I say, "So, like, you had no sleep at all, right? You don't know it, but you called me up around two A.M. Chicago time. So it was after three o'clock in New York, and I heard you, still wide awake, arguing with some guy."

"What? What are you talking about?"

The sudden sharpness in his voice is a surprise, so I laugh a little and say, "You must have sat on your phone, 'cause it dialed my number in the middle of the night."

"And, like . . . you heard all that?" He's trying to sound neutral now, calm. But he's upset about this.

"No," I say. "I just heard a little—enough to catch the tone, that's all."

"And the tone was . . . ?"

Again, the sharpness. And now he's starting to irritate me. "Like I said—it sounded like an argument, that's all. Nothing specific. It's not a big deal. But if you don't want people to eavesdrop, try turning off your phone before you sit on it."

"So you *were* eavesdropping, right?"

The elevator doors open, and Gertie leads me out and takes a sharp right. She knows we're going to the room I always reserve. So does Bobby.

I take a deep breath and let it out slowly. "Look, I was sound asleep. My phone buzzed, and I knew it was you, so I answered, and I heard some talking for about ten seconds. And, yes, I listened. Which is not a crime. End of story, all right? I was only saying that you must not have gotten much sleep, remember? Just a friendly observation, that's all. Friendly."

He laughs and takes my hand again. But now it feels forced.

"Sorry," he says. "You're right. Not enough sleep, I guess. Didn't mean to snap at you."

We're walking along the railing at the stairwell to the floor below, and he says, "Hey, guess what. My parents are away until Sunday. Dad's talking at some particle physics conference in Switzerland, and Mom went with. No school till Monday, no parents around . . . now, if I could just find somebody really *nice* to hang out with . . . Too bad you didn't let me pet your dog."

The cheeriness still feels forced, but I smile and play along. "Very funny."

"So, you want to come over? For the afternoon, maybe stay and eat some dinner?"

He's asking me to come and be alone with him.

But I'm confused, and I don't answer, pretending to concentrate on navigation.

" 'Cause the fridge is full of food. It'll be good to have some time to catch up."

He wants me to come, he's asking again. And we can be alone, and I can talk to him. Because I have to.

But now it feels odd. Because I don't know what's going on between us. I want to spend time with him. I do. I need to. But something still tells me to hold back.

Because *he's* holding back. About what happened in New York. And about that conversation I heard last night. Why would he do that? And after I say what I have to say to him, then what? And look at us—we can't even talk for three minutes without arguing.

Tootsie, Tootsie, Tootsie—overanalyzing! What is your problem? Just smile and say, "Great—when should I come over?"

But I can't say that.

I say, "I've got a lot to get done right now—for school. Can I see how the work goes, and call you a little later?"

A one-second delay, just enough to tell me he's surprised. But he hides it.

"Sure, fine. I mean, I'm just barging into your day out of nowhere. Absolutely."

And he lets go of my hand.

We're at the door of room 307, a music-listening room where my talking laptop won't bother anyone. It's the same room where Bobby found me two years ago. Where we had our second conversation. A century ago.

I'm sure he's remembering all the time we've spent here. Because I am. It's not only that early conversation that happened in here. This room has been one of our sanctuaries. One of our hideouts.

He touches me on the arm, and he's close enough for me to smell the toothpaste on his breath. "So, call me, okay?"

I smile, nod. "I will. And thanks for coming to see me, Bobby."

"Good to be home. See you later, Alicia."

I nod. "Unless I see you first." One of our oldest jokes.

A little laugh from each of us, and he's gone.

I'm in the room now, and the heavy door hisses shut, and it's completely quiet. Soundproof. I release Gertie, and I hear her move to the corner, walk around in a circle a few times, and then lie down and heave a big sigh. She's off duty. Nap time.

Me, I'm wide-awake in the dark, hyperconscious, leaning forward, both hands on the cold oak tabletop. And I'm replaying every second since the moment Bobby said my name out in the library courtyard. Thinking of all the warm, funny, intelligent things I could have said.

But didn't.

Something feels so wrong, so empty, so . . . lost. Again.

But this time it's the kind of lost where I feel the dense darkness closing in around me. The heavy stuff. Suffocating me. Drowning me. Cramming me into a coffin, a premature burial, bleak as Poe, black as a raven. Nevermore.

But I know what to do when it gets this dark. I have experience with blindtime. And wounds.

So first I make myself sit.

I make my mind be still.

I make my mind make my body be still.

I breathe. Long, deep breaths.

And then I listen to my heart.

Not the thumping one. My other heart.

The heart that knows the deep things.

The heart that knows that the light is real.

The heart that knows that the darkness is only light's absence.

The heart that has already recovered from sadness far deeper than this.

And I know that now I must *do*.

Doing is important.

Doing is evidence, proof that I'm alive, intact, still myself.

Because a girl who is drowned in darkness does not sit down at the library table and light up her computer.

A girl in a coffin does not find her audio notes and listen as her own voice tells her what to do next.

A dead girl does not wipe her eyes and open a new document and begin tapping ideas into focus, making the words obey her.

And as my doing does its work, now the heart that does not thump knows that nothing important has changed.

And this heart tells me that soon I'll make that phone call to Bobby. I will. I'll call my friend. And my friend will answer. And I'll talk with my friend.

Friend.

It's a bright word, and I hold it tight.

chapter 5

watchers

I t's going to be colder walking home. The forecast said it's going down to five degrees tonight.

So I sit on the bench across from the front door security desk at the library and tie my scarf behind my neck so it covers my nose and chin. It's a nuisance, and I know it makes me look like a bank robber, but when it's way below freezing and I've got to walk due north, it's not about fashion. It's about survival.

"Miss, may I have a word with you?"

It's a British accent spoken by a man who's standing up, about two feet to my right.

I turn toward the voice and give a neutral smile. Which is stupid, because I've got a scarf across my face. I pull the scarf down and say, "Sure."

Gertie's been sitting to my left, and she stands up and leans against my knee. And then she growls.

She never does that.

"Gertie, down. *Down.* Good girl. You'll have to pardon her manners."

"Not at all. She's a beautiful dog. I've never owned a

shepherd, but one day I'd like to. One of the brightest breeds is what I hear. And excellent as guide dogs. Have you had her a long time?"

I smile and give Gertie a pat on her head. "No, only about six months. And she's the smartest dog I've ever known. And she learns really fast too."

The man's not moving toward Gertie, not trying to pet her or anything, so that's good. And I'm thinking our conversation is over. It was a dog chat.

Then he says, "There's something else I need to tell you."

Goose bumps. Up and down both my arms. It's his voice. He's dropped it low, almost a whisper. I know this tone. People use it for telling secrets.

He says, "I think your friend, the young man who came into the library with you earlier, I think he may be in danger. Considerable danger."

I feel him take a seat on the bench to my right. I'm short of breath. "I . . . I don't understand."

Gertie sits up, leans against me again. She can tell I'm afraid. Another low growl. "Gertie, hush—*hush*. Good girl. Like, have you been *watching* me?"

"No, not at all. Not you. Your friend. I've been watching him. And watching the two other people who are also watching him, the two that I've spotted. There may be others. And now that he's had contact with you, someone could be watching you as well. Right now."

In a flash I recognize this voice. "Fee, fie, foe, fum"— it was an Englishman arguing with Bobby in my dream this morning. But I didn't hear this man's voice in a dream. It's a real voice. I heard him speak during a phone call. Last night, when I was eavesdropping.

I whisper, "You and Bobby talked last night, about three in the morning, right?" I don't know why I'm whispering.

"Ah—so he told you about that. It was closer to four. And yes, we had a talk. More like a shouting match. And he jumped into a cab with his suitcase before I got to tell him what I think is happening, before I convinced him how much I need his help. I've got to make him understand what's going on."

And even though I've got my hat and coat on, I shiver. Because I'm picking up this deep agitation, almost a hunger in the man's voice. And I'm hearing desperation too, the same kind I've heard in the voices of kids I've tutored at the Hadley School, kids who can't face the fact that they're not going to see again. This man's in trouble.

But I jump back to what he just told me.

"Bobby," I say. "He doesn't know these people are watching him?"

"No, I don't think so. There are two men. They're very . . . professional."

And the way he says it, the word *professional* sounds like a threat.

"But . . . why? And why are *you* watching—who are you?"

"My name is . . . William. And if you are who I think

you are, your friend may have told you about me. About finding me in New York City."

My heart almost stops, then starts pounding so I can feel each beat in my neck, in my arms, on my wrists. Because Bobby did tell me a little. He said he'd found someone in New York, a man who'd had the same experience he had. A man who woke up one morning and couldn't see his body. A man who is sitting next to me. In the library. In Chicago. Right now.

And I want to leave, run away, get as far from this man as I can. But I can't. Because if Bobby's involved, so am I.

And that means that I have to know if this man really is who I think he is. And there's only one way I can find out.

I reach out my right hand, and I whisper, "Please— put your arm here." He does, and I touch, and I can judge how far away he's sitting by his forearm, and his elbow, and the angle of his upper arm. It's a thin arm, all muscle. Then I open my hand and push it toward him.

And my palm hits bare flesh—a bony rib cage, zero body fat.

He's not wearing a shirt.
no shirt
in the library
he's right . . . here
on this bench
no one else can see him—no one else knows he's here
except Gertie

I yank my hand back.

This man is why Bobby told Gwen our secret. About turning invisible.

My legs are shaking, and I feel my face go pale. Gertie sits up, moves closer, leans against my knees.

And this man is completely naked. He has to be. It's the only way he could be out in public.

This happened to me before. Two years ago it was Bobby, invisible and out in public, and me there, facing the same facts. That was the first time. But past experience does not make a skinny, naked, invisible Englishman any less weird. Or disturbing.

Gertie growls again.

"Gertie, hush. Good girl. Sorry," I say to him, "I mean, about pushing you like that. I had to . . . see." I'm still whispering.

"No apologies needed. You're Alicia, right? Alicia Van Dorn?" I nod, and he says, "I heard Robert speaking about his girlfriend when he was in New York. And he mentioned she was blind."

Robert. That's what Bobby's been calling himself. Says it's his professional name. It's what Gwen calls him. And even though I've got a million questions whizzing through my head, all I want to ask this man is what Bobby—what Robert—said. When he was speaking about me. About his girlfriend. When he was in New York.

But I say, "Why is Bobby being followed?"

"Because of me. And because of this . . . condition

we've both had." Again, I can hear the desperation in his voice. "I had a tangle with the police in New York, and I managed to get away. But not before a young officer got a grip on my arm for a few seconds, just long enough to become extremely upset by what he was seeing. Or rather, *not* seeing. And now the authorities in New York are struggling with an impossible concept—that there's a transparent man on the loose in Manhattan, possibly more than one. And possibly elsewhere as well. And that scares them, as it jolly well should. And I'm certain there's a huge push to get to the bottom of it. An invisible-man hunt."

As he's talking, I've got this sudden urge to get rid of this man, like maybe chain him to a concrete block and dump him off a pier. Not that I'd do that. But the thought comes anyway. Because it sounds like he's inches away from exposing this secret, which would be awful for Bobby. Awful for me too. Because if this takes one wrong turn, the government will take him. Or the spymasters will get him. Or the physicists and the biologists. Someone will take him, because Bobby is Exhibit A, the living proof that a human being can vanish from sight and then come back. And for anyone who sees the world as an us-and-them sort of place, invisibility offers an irresistible power. I've had a long time to think about this, about the explosive effect this information could have if it gets loose, and not just on our own private lives— Bobby's and mine and our families'. We'll just be the early casualties.

I push the grim thoughts away, try to refocus on the immediate problem. And I ask, "So . . . what's Bobby got to do with all of it, I mean with you and the police? You're the one they're after, right? I still don't get why these people are watching *him*."

"Yes, well, that's the sad bit. Robert and I? We got off to a very bad start when we first met in New York, and I'm to blame for a big part of that. And he . . ."

Footsteps. On the tile floor, moving toward me from the right, then shuffling to a stop in front of me.

A tall man with a deep voice clears his throat. "Excuse me, miss, I'm Officer Dennison, U of C Security. Are you all right? Can I offer some assistance?"

I smile as best I can, tilting my face toward his voice. "No, I'm fine. Just bundling up before I head for home."

"Good, 'cause it's cold out there. Have you got a long walk? I could get a university patrol car here right away. Be happy to help out."

"No, I'll be fine, thanks. It's only about seven blocks. I come here all the time."

"Oh, I know. I've seen you a lot. Well, sorry to bother you. Have a good afternoon, all right?"

I smile and nod. "Thanks again."

I begin gathering my things again—find my gloves, then readjust my scarf, get to my feet, put the strap of my bag over my right shoulder, and I hear the officer walking back toward the security desk. Poor guy. He got worried, watching the blind girl nodding and talking to herself. I don't blame him. And I bet he's still got an eye on me.

"Gertie, come . . . good girl."

We start for the doors, and she's nervous as a sparrow. But we're on the move, leaving, and she's glad.

Not me. Because I need to ask that man more questions. About what happened with him and the police. About why he's here in Chicago. About the men following Bobby. And about that other thing. What Robert said about me. His girlfriend.

I'm straining my ears, hoping to hear a whisper from William.

It doesn't come.

And a minute later Gertie and I are through the double doors, across the courtyard, and headed for home, walking into a biting wind. And I know that man is not going to be anywhere near us now, not in this cold. Not without clothes.

So my questions will have to wait.

And other things will have to wait as well. Probably.

Because about an hour ago, I did call Bobby—after I worked on my history project. And after more scolding from my inner voice. And Bobby's picking me up in about an hour and we're going over to his house. We've got a date. We're going to be alone.

And after that phone call an hour ago, I had it all worked out in my mind. How Bobby and I would find the perfect moment. How we'd sit close together, how we'd talk. Finally.

But now I have to tell him about William. And about the people who are shadowing him.

Because even if I hate it, and even if Bobby and I never get to be truly alone, and even if it means that my heart shrivels up and dies, I still have to deal with things as they are . . . right? Right.

And the way things are at the moment is rotten.

Because that feeling I've been having, that everything's at risk? It's not a feeling anymore. It's a certainty.

chapter 6

orbits

I'm on Ellis Avenue, a little more than halfway home. Physically.

Mentally, I'm bouncing all over the place. I'm in New York, trying to understand what happened there. I'm in the middle of three or four imaginary conversations with Bobby. And I'm back at the library questioning the Englishman. Who is naked. And invisible.

I'm handling that particular circumstance pretty well, I think. Dealing with it calmly, rationally.

If I weren't blind, I know I'd be having a more severe reaction to that man. But disembodied voices are nothing new to me. I *understand* William is invisible, but I can only imagine how others can't see him. Actually not seeing him with my own eyes would be more of a shock. That's my theory. Plus, I'm one of the few people on earth who has experience in this field—maybe I should have included that as a skill on my college applications: Perfectly at ease with invisible people.

Because I'm not frightened by this man. I'm more

scared about the people following Bobby. Because I don't believe they're really after *him*, at least not yet. The police want to get to the bottom of their encounter with William, and there must be some way they think following Bobby will help with that. That's what I think. Because they definitely want to find William. Because as far as they're concerned, either a weird and very dangerous phenomenon is for real, *or* they've just got a very crazy New York police officer on their hands—the one who reported that he had his hands around the arm of an invisible man.

So really, the main thing is to keep William from being caught.

Because if they get to William, they'll want Bobby too. Because he's taken the round-trip. And they'll also want to round up anyone else who knows anything at all about the phenomenon. Which includes me, my parents, and Bobby's parents. And Gwen, the newest member of our little club.

But my thoughts are just chasing themselves around in circles. I need facts. And I need Bobby.

I've already reached for my phone four times, to tell him people are watching him. But it's not like he's doing anything suspicious or illegal. If I tell him he's being followed, he might start acting weird or something.

And he might not want to come over and pick me up. For our date. To go to his house.

I haven't figured out what happens if my mom's home, what I'm going to tell her about going out this afternoon. She's not a big Bobby fan. That can probably be traced to the day two years ago when he showed up naked at our front door. Invisible, yes, but naked. Not a good first impression.

Because back then, if Bobby wanted to get out of his house, he had to bundle up, completely cover his body and face. Or do the opposite—like the Englishman I just met.

Mom won't like me going over to Bobby's. Of course, she probably doesn't know his parents are away. And if she doesn't ask, I don't have to tell her. That's my rule. I try not to lie, but I don't require myself to volunteer sensitive information.

. . . *five, six, seven, eight* . . .

I've got this meter in my head that's always counting steps, always keeping myself located on a mental grid. I've turned left onto Fifty-fifth Street now, and I've got about 220 steps straight ahead to reach Drexel Avenue.

Bobby tells me all the time how great MapQuest is, and how Google Earth is so amazing. And I'm sure he's right. But I have to make my own maps.

Sometimes late at night when I can't sleep, I walk through our house in my mind, then I go out for a mental walk. I walk south on Ellis toward the university, noticing my place markers—the smell of the asphalt from the big parking lot at Fifty-fifth Street; the smell of bleach from the laundry dryer vents at the university gym; the little dog with the high-pitched voice who barks at Gertie and me from a ground floor window of the Young Building; loud music from the dorms in the commons. When I cross Fifty-seventh Street, I take a few turns around the main quads, find my favorite stone archways with the deepest echoes, listen for the chimes from the bell tower at the Rockefeller Chapel. And when I'm good and tired, I use my mental compass and I find my way home. I go in the front door, climb the stairs, turn right, go past the bathroom, find my own door, and climb back into the bed I've never left.

. . . *eighty-five, eighty-six, eighty-seven* . . .

And whenever I walk, for real or not, I feel how my world has shrunk, and I fight that, every day, every second. I refuse to let the whole wide universe become a few small maps folded up inside my head. Because everything keeps trying to collapse inward, the way a dying star goes dense and dark. The gravity grabs all the light. No escape.

But I'm fighting it. And I'm ambitious: I'm going to bring all that brightness back inside. I'm going to include it all. In my consciousness. Which is the only place it ever was anyway. Deep philosophy, right here on Fifty-fifth Street.

And I'm not kidding myself. All this mental chitchat is just to keep myself from worrying about invisible men and professional stalkers. And Bobby. And the whole newsreel drama of my life.

Gertie's calmed down. A close encounter with a person who smells and moves and talks, but who *looks* all wrong—can't blame her for getting edgy. And the more

I think about that man, the less I trust him. There was something in his voice that scared me. Maybe the desperation. Because a person who's truly desperate can be dangerous. And dishonest. And volatile.

But Gertie's put that behind her now, and she's just marching ahead. Wish I could say the same. When I grow up, I want to be as mature and stable and single-minded as my dog.

The steps have been stepped and the turns have been turned, and as I open our front gate, I hear the squeak of the top hinge. The picket fence along the sidewalk was Dad's idea to help me distinguish our front walk from the others on this side of the street.

Up the stairs, open the storm door, take the key out of my bag, find the lock, turn the key and the knob, step into the entryway, and then reach up on the wall to the alarm panel and punch the code before the thirty seconds are up. Which isn't easy when my fingers are this cold. "System is armed."

"Hi . . . I'm home. . . ." My voice echoes up the front staircase. No answer.

Good. Mom's not here. Which means I might not have to face an inquisition before I go to Bobby's. If I can get out of here fast enough.

I unclip the handle from Gertie's harness, hang it on the hook by the tall mirror. Released from duty, Gertie trots back toward the kitchen. Then I put my computer bag on the little bench in the front hallway, put my gloves and hat and scarf on the table beside it. I hang my coat on its hanger and shut the closet door. A place for everything, and everything in its place. Hook, bench, table, hanger. My life depends on knowing exactly where everything is.

Which is another reason that William's arrival is so upsetting. The newness, the unpredictability—that's almost more troubling than the invisibility. Because he's in our orbit now, mine and Bobby's, floating around like an asteroid or a chunk of space debris. Something else to bump into.

Talking to Bobby ought to help. He can put a few more things in order for me, help me find a hook for hanging up an invisible Englishman.

But not yet. Right now? I'm pushing it all out of my mind. Again.

I want to go up to my room and get ready, maybe shower, change outfits. Because I have a date. And something wonderful could still happen. It's possible.

I'm holding on to that. My so-called date with Bobby. Today.

No matter what.

chapter 7

gentleman caller

obby always says I look great, but he doesn't know I work at it. Not obsessively or anything. Just enough. Blindness and vanity—bad combination. And this afternoon will be the first time we've spent any time alone together in ages.

I'm going to go upstairs and take a shower and stop thinking about everything except Bobby.

And I know I'm being stupid, getting all prettied up. But I'm going to anyway. And I'm going to wear my dark green cashmere sweater and my new tan wool slacks. Maybe even risk a little blush on my winter-pale cheeks. I'm sure I look like a ghost.

Looks. Like I can afford to be worrying about my looks.

But first things first.

Because before *anything* else happens, Gertie needs a meal. And then she needs to go out. She's on a special diet that helps regulate how often she needs to do her business. Which seems gross, but me knowing exactly what she needs is part of our deal. She's been right at my side for the past three hours, being my eyes, taking care of me. So now it's my turn. Symbiosis.

I get to the kitchen, and I already know where Gertie is. She's lying down with her nose aimed at her big porcelain bowl, ready for the food ritual.

And after I've got the kibbles in the bowl, and added a cup of hot water, and stirred it with a spoon, I straighten up and say, "All right, Gertie. Food."

She waits until I say that. She'd wait all day, with the meal right there in front of her nose. Once I forgot to give her permission. Daddy came home at nine P.M. and she was lying there, looking at her food. Only happened once.

And thinking of Daddy makes me wonder again about all those visits from Dr. Phillips, Bobby's dad. All that time they've spent out back in the study. I asked Daddy once what they were working on, and he said it was university business, a joint project of the astronomy and the physics departments. Which makes sense, I guess.

I sit down at the table and listen to Gertie. Fifteen or twenty seconds of furious eating, and mealtime is over. She's beginning to lick the bowl. The last part of the ritual is a trip to the backyard, but before I get up from my chair, the front doorbell rings.

Gertie's claws skitter on the tile as she bolts past me, through the door and along the hallway, light on her feet for a German shepherd. But she doesn't bark. She never barks.

Probably Bobby. Twenty minutes early for a date. A good sign. Except I haven't had time to shower and change. Guess I have to let that go.

I follow my head map along the hallway wall, past the library doors on the right, past the living room doorway on the left, then right to the front staircase banister to get my bearings, and then eight steps straight across the front hall. Gertie whines softly, almost a yawn, to help me find her. I pat her head, and she's sitting to the left of the vestibule door, patient and sweet, her nose just below the doorknob.

The bell rings again, and I can picture him there, maybe a little nervous, a shy smile on his lips.

And when I open the door, I'm going to act completely normal, even though I know people are watching him. Watching us.

I'm through the vestibule door, then two steps, and I put a hand against the door that opens onto the front porch. Gertie sniffs at the frame.

I'm sure it's Bobby, but I never just open the door.

"Hello?" The door's thick, so I talk loud.

"Good afternoon, ma'am. I'm with the FBI, Special Agent Charles Porter. I need to talk with the parents of Alicia Van Dorn. If you'll take a look through the peephole in the door there, I'm holding up my badge and my photo ID for you."

It's a deep voice, confident and official. The voice of a man who carries a gun. The voice of a man with massive reinforcements at his command.

My heart's beating so fast, I can barely speak.

"I . . . I'm sorry, but her parents aren't home."

A two-second pause. The man says, "Miss, are you Alicia Van Dorn?"

I gulp, and I imagine he heard it, right through the door. And I say, "Yes, I am." My voice is shaky, and I reach down and put my left hand on Gertie's head. She leans against my leg. She's not scared at all.

"Can you tell me when your parents will be home? If it's possible, I need to stop back today or tonight and speak with all three of you."

"I . . . I don't know when they'll be home. It could be any minute." Which is true. Sometimes Mom is home by mid-afternoon on Thursday. And Dad too. And sometimes they both get busy and I don't see anyone until dinnertime. Or later.

I hear the latch of the storm door, hear it open, then the hinges chirp and the latch clicks shut again. "Miss, I've put my card inside the storm door, and I've circled my cell phone number. Please ask one of your parents to call me as soon as possible, all right?"

I say, "Yes, sir. I'll tell them."

"Thanks." Then a second later the voice says, "And you did the right thing, miss, not opening the door to a stranger. Have a good afternoon."

His footsteps cross the porch, go down the steps. And the top hinge on the gate squeaks.

I'm back in the hallway, pushing the vestibule door shut, glad to lean against it, get my breath back. The FBI wants to talk to me. And my parents. We're going to have an official interview. With the Federal Bureau of Investigation. We're being investigated. All of us.

And I wonder if they're trying to get in touch with Bobby's dad too. Because we're all in this. All of us.

Bobby—now I've got to call him.

But can I do that? I mean, safely? Because if the FBI is on a case, don't they tap the phones, listen in?

Doesn't matter. I *have* to call him.

And I've got my phone out. Flip, scroll, select, dial. Bobby picks up in the middle of the first ring.

There's music blasting, the Beatles, "A Hard Day's Night." It stops, and he says, "Hi, I'm close—be there in five minutes, maybe less. Meet you out front?"

"Um . . . no. Come to the garage door back in the alley, okay? And I'll let you in."

"But I thought we were—"

I cut in, "See you there, okay?"

And I hang up.

One of the last movies I ever saw in a theater was *Enemy of the State*. I know it's not smart to base any thinking on stuff I saw in a Will Smith movie about a huge invasion of privacy by the U.S. government, but I can't help feeling like there are satellites overhead taking high-resolution pictures of my neighborhood. And agents with binoculars out front in a white van. And other agents with headphones, recording everything. And they're all wearing dark suits and dark glasses.

"Gertie, come." I take the harness handle from its hook by the mirror and clip it on. And right away I feel better. No matter what resources Special Agent Charles Porter has, *I've* got Gertie.

And now my dog and I are going to walk to the back of the house, then down the four steps from the kitchen, across the small landing, then up four steps to another door, the one on the right that opens into the covered walkway that leads out back to my dad's study—twelve steps—then we'll walk straight across his study—ten steps—and through the opposite door into the walkway that connects to the garage—fourteen steps. It's a lot longer than just going out the back door and across the yard to the garage. But it's a more secure path. And it's more hidden. And I think it's what I should do in this kind of situation.

Except I don't know what kind of situation this is . . . do I?

No.

But it's time to stop thinking. Time to do.

And I say, "Gertie, forward."

And I give myself the same command: *Alicia, forward.*

It's the only way to go. In this kind of situation.

chapter 8

squeaks

There are two cars in this world I can positively identify by sound: my dad's rumbly old Saab convertible and Bobby's Volvo station wagon—which is even rumblier and clankier and squeakier.

After waiting in the garage for a minute or so, I hear the Volvo and I push the button that lifts the wide door onto the alley. It's a big garage, so there's room for Bobby to pull in next to our car. When the engine stops, I push the button again, and the door grinds its way back down.

The car door groans open, and Bobby says, "How come you shut the garage? Aren't we going to my house?"

He's out of the car and standing beside me.

"I hope so," I say, "but first we have to talk."

He takes my hand. "I know."

And I have no idea what he means. But he's got my complete attention.

Then Bobby says, "I . . . I acted like a real jerk, you

know, back at the library. I wanted that to be a lot . . . different than it turned out, more . . . more friendly and everything. And I'm sorry." He pauses, brushes the hair away from my face. "So, yeah, let's talk, okay?"

And I could scream, because this is the perfect beginning for the kind of talk I want us to have. About how we feel. About each other. And we can't. Not yet.

So I say, "Bobby, I'm so glad you said that, because I felt awful. After you left the library. And I want to talk too, about . . . everything. But some other stuff happened, just in the last hour or so. And it's serious."

"What? What do you mean?" he says. "You're not . . . like, sick or something, are you?" And there's almost a quaver in his voice.

I squeeze his hand. "No, no, it's nothing like that. It's William. I had a talk with William."

"William? William who?"

"The man from New York. The man you were arguing with at three o'clock this morning."

Bobby takes a step back, lets go of my hand.

"No way! He *called* you? But . . . like, how did he get your number?"

"He didn't call. He's here in Chicago, Bobby. He came up to me in the library and started talking. About forty minutes ago. Said that he's seen two men following you, said he thought you were in danger. He said someone is probably watching me too."

Bobby pushes a quick breath out between his lips. "This is . . . this is bad—what else did he say?"

"That was about it. We got cut off because a security guard came over and talked to me. And it gets even worse, because just a few minutes ago an FBI agent came to the front door."

"*No way! The FBI? Here!*"

I nod. "Yeah, and he wants to talk to me and my mom and dad—they're not home now. We're supposed to call him later."

Gertie whines softly, nudges my leg. I forgot—poor thing, she still needs to go out. So I take off the harness handle and open the door to the backyard. "Okay, Gertie, good girl."

I shut the door and turn back to Bobby.

I lift one eyebrow, and I say, "So . . . what do you think? What's going on? And what should we do?"

"I . . ." He hesitates, and then starts over, speaking slowly. "First of all, I'm so sorry that you're getting pulled into all of this. Again. I didn't want that to happen."

He sounds small. And tired. And his voice has a tenderness I haven't heard for a long time.

"Because I really messed up. *That's* what's going on. I set something in motion, and I have no idea how it's going to end. And it's all because I saw this guy's shadow in a store in New York, and I should have just turned away, pretended not to see him. But I didn't. I stared."

I'm hugging my arms—it's freezing here in the garage. "Let's go talk in the house, okay? We can walk through my dad's study."

I could call Gertie in, clip the handle back onto her

harness, and have her guide me. Or I could easily walk back into the house without my dog, without any help at all.

But I want to be helped.

"Could I hold your arm?"

"Sure." Bobby steps ahead of me, and I put my right hand above his left elbow. And he moves his arm, hugging my hand against his side. He's wearing a fleece jacket, too light for a day this cold. I feel the warmth of his arm through the fabric.

As he opens the door into the walkway, he says, "How did William sound to you? I mean, besides British. Did he seem strange or anything? Or even, like, dangerous? 'Cause when I first met him in New York, I thought he was a real creep, a genuine psycho. Which is why I got the police involved."

"Really?" The word comes out like a gasp. Because I'm shocked. Two years ago we were so careful to keep everything about the invisibility a complete secret—especially from the authorities.

He says, "I mean, I didn't tell them exactly what to look for or anything, but I needed William to back off, leave me alone. So I told the police where to find his neighborhood. And that he was great at disguising himself."

"You told them that?" Again, I'm surprised.

"Yeah," he says, and I can hear the regret in his voice. "Because it felt like my only choice. I was afraid he was going to start hurting people, or maybe take a hostage or something, try to force me to tell him how the whole process works. And I knew I couldn't tell him that. So I told the police to watch out for him, just to give him something else to worry about. And I wish I hadn't, because it didn't go the way I planned. I didn't think things would loop back to me. Or to you. And I'm really sorry about that."

Again, the tenderness. I squeeze his arm a little, and I say, "It's okay. We'll just have to deal with it. But about you and him and the police and what happened in New York—I think he was starting to tell me about that in the library, before we got cut off. But, really, he didn't sound creepy to me. Desperate, yes. And scared that the police are after him—except I don't think he's sure the police actually know anything about the invisibility, or even if any of them believe the whole invisibility thing is for real."

"Really?" Bobby says. "Why do you say that?"

"Because William said that one policeman had hold of his arm for about ten seconds, and then he got loose, got away clean. And that's the only actual contact he's had with anyone at the NYPD."

"That is *huge* news." There's a gush of relief in Bobby's voice. Then more soberly, he adds, "If it's true. Because if there's only one policeman saying he had his hands around some invisible guy, I bet the cops called a psychiatrist, not a physicist. Which means we might still be able to keep the whole thing bottled up. Unless William does something really stupid, like getting himself caught. Or attacking someone. And you're sure you didn't get a bad vibe when you were talking to him?"

I shake my head. "He's really tense, and I got this undercurrent of desperation, but I think he's mostly scared. That's the feeling I got. And I think he honestly wanted to help, to warn you about the men following you."

Bobby opens the door into my dad's study, and he says, "See, that's what I don't get—why this guy's being so nicey-nice all of a sudden. Because when we talked last night in New York, he even apologized for the way he'd acted at first, said we had to work together now, said he's trying to help me, and of course, he wants me to help him. But he was *not* like that when he showed up at Gwen's house in the city. He'd seen me spot his shadow, and then he followed us home, silently, right into her living room. Threatened us, really scared us. All that could have been an act, I guess. But I don't get it."

We're halfway across the study when Bobby stops.

He says, "What, is your dad keeping pets back here? Hermit crabs? Or hamsters?"

"No, I don't think so."

"So . . . what are the little cages for?"

"Cages? Really? I haven't been in this room for months. Your dad's been back here a lot more than I have."

"My dad? What do you mean?" he asks.

"The two of them have been working on something

for the university, my dad said. A joint project of the physics department and the astronomy department. So, what are these cages like?"

And I'm picturing the way I remember this room from years ago—about twenty feet long and fifteen feet wide, Daddy's big desk near the garage end, bookcases lining both walls, an Oriental rug on the floor, a long oak table covered with stacks of scientific journals, and no windows except for the three skylights.

"Here," he says, "take a look. The table's got a lot of other stuff on it, all sorts of electrical stuff, so be careful." And Bobby guides my hands to the oak table, and then to a clear space near the center.

And what we have are small glass aquariums with wire mesh tops, three of them side by side.

"And they're empty?" I ask.

"Yup. Just wood shavings. And little food pellets. And some tiny poop. Nice."

"Shh," I say. "What's that?"

"What?" he asks.

I lean down closer to one of the cages—little scratching sounds. "Hear it now?"

"Yeah," he says. "Give the cage a shake."

I do, and Bobby gasps.

"Alicia!"

"What?" And I hear him slide the two other cages around on the table, then the sound of scrabbling claws and little high-pitched squeaks. An involuntary shiver runs through me.

"Those squeaks?" he says. "And the tiny droppings? There are *mice* in these cages, in all three of them."

"Down under the shavings?"

"Yeah," Bobby says, "and now up on top, moving around."

I'm confused. "You mean, like, little lab mice?"

"Exactly," he says, "the kind used for experiments."

"But my dad's not that kind of a scientist, never was."

"Well, he is now," Bobby says, "because these little guys have been worked on."

"You mean they're, like . . . *deformed* or something? Bobby, that's horrible!"

"No," he says, "not deformed. At least I don't think so. But I can't really tell. All these mice? They're invisible."

chapter 9

tissue

I feel around until I find Daddy's desk and then his chair. I have to sit down.

My dad. Running a research lab in our back-yard. Experimenting on mice. Creating invisible squeakers. Frankenmice.

Everything is coming unglued. I can't think what to say about it. And I'm surprised by the first words out of my mouth.

"Bobby, your dad is in on this."

He says, "What? What do you mean?"

"He's been at our house at least five times in the past couple months, and every time, the two of them have been out here for three or four hours. And now we know what they've been up to." I wave toward the cages. "*That* is their big joint project. It has to be."

I wait, but Bobby doesn't try to argue. Because the puzzle pieces fit together too tightly. And I want to jump up and grab Bobby's hand so we can run to the garage, get in his car, and drive over to his house. We'll pull the shades, lock the doors, smash our cell phones. We'll build a fire in the fireplace, curl up on the floor, and the two of us will talk for hours and hours as the flames burn to embers. Then we'll doze off, warm in each other's arms. And we'll wake up and realize all of this was just a bad dream.

But it's not. It's happening. This phenomenon. The cold, hard physics. And I have to deal with things as they are, we both do.

I take a deep breath, let it out. And I say, "So . . . why are they doing this?"

A long pause before Bobby answers. "No idea. Unless it's like they . . ."

Footsteps. In the walkway from the house. Coming fast.

My instinct is to rush back the way we came, hide in the garage. But I'm no good at rushing anywhere.

The door opens, and Bobby says, "Dr. Van Dorn . . . um, hi."

I make an attempt at a smile toward the doorway. "Hi, Daddy." And as guilty and confused as I sound, I'm so glad it's him. I imagined those footsteps belonging to William. Or the FBI. Or a terrorist.

There's an awkward wedge of silence—nothing but tiny mouse scratchings.

Daddy clears his throat. "Well. It looks like you've met our little friends there. I'm glad you know about this now, both of you. Because I haven't liked keeping this hidden. The only other person who knows is Bobby's father. And both our wives. And neither of your mothers have been happy about this, none of us are. But we all understand why it's been important to move ahead with the research."

I know this tone of voice I'm hearing. It's the same voice Daddy used when I was five and he explained why I couldn't talk to strangers. Or chase a ball into the street. Or climb out my bedroom window onto the front porch roof. It's his danger voice, the one that means, "Don't argue, because I know I'm right about this."

And as he begins to talk, it sounds like he's been ready to explain this for a long time. Because he's got his major points all lined up. He knew this moment would come.

"Dr. Phillips and I began tracking research on this subject in the scientific journals two years ago, right after Bobby's experience. This is a hot area in applied physics right now—they call it cloaking technology. And it's being funded by the military and intelligence communities in at least five different countries, which is a very disturbing fact."

Daddy's beginning to pace on the carpet, three steps one way, turn, and come back. I know this pattern. He's working the logic, putting his lecture together.

"And there's about a hundred million dollars' worth of ongoing research—and those are just the published figures. They're trying to figure out how to hide things like planes and satellites and military installations. But they're focused on specific materials that deflect waves, materials that let waves—radar or microwaves, for example—slip around them instead of bouncing off, sort of the way the materials in the B-2 stealth bomber deflected radar waves. And recently the research has extended to the visible light spectrum—to develop a material that will let normal light waves slip by with no reflection, which would make anything beneath it invisible."

A salesman, that's what Daddy reminds me of. He wants us to buy in. He needs us to agree.

He says, "But Bobby's experience? That was actual molecular-level light management, or at least that's what we're calling it. To have *living tissue* stop reflecting light? That is very different from making an inert material do that. And we have to assume others are also working on this. Don't you see? To think we can keep this idea hidden, it just isn't realistic. And in terms of pure science, when something like this pops into view, it can't be ignored. It would have been irresponsible not to try to understand it. And it would be even more irresponsible if we didn't try to be prepared for the worst case: which would be a person or a group of people who want to use this knowledge to harm others, to create terror and instability. We're doing our work from a humanitarian perspective, and with a global view, and it's purely defensive. And we're documenting everything we're doing. Just in case. But the work has to be done. We have no choice. I hope you can see that."

I don't know if Bobby is nodding his head in agreement. Or looking skeptical. Or if he's stunned and outraged by Daddy's speech. Because it was *his* experience. And it's been hijacked.

Me, I'm trying to keep my face neutral. Because I don't know how I feel about this. It makes me want to ask Daddy if he and Dr. Phillips have started writing their acceptance speeches for the Nobel Prize. It makes me want to ask how the mice are doing—are they having invisible mouse babies? Any nasty side effects that Bobby and William should know about? And I have a lot of physics-type questions, a lot of what-ifs too. Because this backyard experimentation, this is another asteroid right here in our home orbit, big and wobbly.

The silence goes on too long, so I say, "I've got an important bit of news for you. An FBI agent came to our front door half an hour ago. He wants to talk to me and you and Mom."

"Are . . . are you *serious*?"

This might be the first time I've ever heard real fear in Daddy's voice. And right away I'm sorry I spoke so casually. And sarcastically.

I nod. "It's true. But I think it's because of what happened to Bobby. In New York last week."

And then Bobby explains how he spotted a shadow man, how the man followed him, overheard him talking about his own invisibility experience, and then demanded information about how to get back to normal. And how the tone got ugly, which made Bobby get the police involved—which ended up with William following Bobby back to Chicago.

I nod, leaning forward in the desk chair. "And I've talked with him, Daddy. He came up to me at the library this afternoon. He wanted me to tell Bobby that he's being followed."

"So . . . they're watching this house, right now? Of course they are—they're tracking a security threat." Daddy's voice goes low and harsh. "Bobby, grab those other two cages and follow me to the kitchen. We don't have much time. If they come in with a warrant, it'll be bad."

I'm lost. "What? What are you doing, Daddy? The kitchen?"

"I've got to put all the mice down the garbage disposal. Sorry, but there's no other way."

I don't like mice, visible or otherwise, but that image is too much. "You can't! Really, Daddy, you *can't*! Maybe . . . maybe we can just let them go or something—no, that wouldn't be good. But to just kill them, Daddy? I'd rather we just called up the FBI, tell them everything. Everything."

"Alicia, the world is not ready for this. Even our own government is not ready for this. Because they'll try to keep it a secret so they can have exclusive use of it."

I feel my eyebrows scrunch together. "But . . . like, that's *good*, isn't it?"

"Maybe," he says, "but probably not. Secrets never

stay that way. And advantages tend to get misused. I am one hundred percent American, but when something gives our side a tactical advantage, it's always temporary, and it almost always ends up biting back. Hard. It's the rule of unintended consequences. Look at nuclear weapons. They ended World War II, but think of the long-term costs. It is an ugly, treacherous world out there. And for this particularly dangerous technology, the defensive solution that Dr. Phillips and I are working on might not be perfect, but it's the best antidote we can think of. Because we *have* to be ready to do something if the secret gets out. That's very clear. And it's urgent. And this secret is *not* getting loose today."

I hear Daddy open the door to the kitchen walkway. The mice start squeaking again as their cages bump around. And I feel like I'm signing off on a death sentence, like it's my duty to fight for a stay of execution.

"But Daddy, is it worth it? All the lying and the sneaking around? Because I'm not seeing it. And that's probably just me. And maybe if you told me the whole idea, this solution you're talking about—"

"Alicia, it's not complicated, we're simply . . ."

He stops. A deep breath, a long sigh.

Then, "I'm sorry, sweetheart, but I can't tell you the details. Because I don't know how this is going to play out, and if anyone questions you or Bobby about *any* of this, both of you have to be able to say 'I don't know'—without committing perjury. You have to trust me on this, okay?"

It's not okay. Nothing's okay.

But I nod at him anyway.

He says, "Bobby, let's go. And then I need to come back here and gather up some files."

And they leave. I hear the footsteps, hear the squeaks fade down the walkway. And before I can hear the distant hiss of water at the kitchen sink, hear the hum and clatter and gargling of the garbage disposal, I jump from Daddy's desk chair and rush across the room, and I trip on the edge of the rug, almost fall. But I get to the door and I slam it shut. Because I can't listen.

I hear it in my imagination anyway. Which is probably worse.

I feel my way back and slump into the chair. And I have my face in my hands, crying real tears. About dead mice.

But it's more than that.

Because I feel the weight of all these interlocking secrets pressing down and down and down, crushing the breath out of me. And *my* secrets—all the things I need to say to Bobby? Also crushed. Slowly suffocating.

And I feel like other things are dying—not just innocent little mice, other things, like dreams, hopes, love—life, liberty, and the pursuit of happiness. Dying, one by one by one.

And I feel like everything is . . . disposable. And a line of poetry jumps into my mind, with a mousy twist: This is the way the world ends, not with a bang, or a whimper, but a squeak.

Excuse me, may I make an observation?

Permission denied. Shut up and go away.

I only want to say that I'm pretty sure this is not the end of the world.

How would you know? Ever been around when the world ended?

Yes, as a matter of fact, I have. And you were there too—remember?

Listen, going blind was *not* the end of the world for me or for anyone else, not by a long shot.

And that, *Henny Penny, is exactly my point.*

Go *away*. Now. And *don't* call me Henny Penny.

I'm already gone. Henny . . . Penny.

Okay. Point taken. The sky is not falling.

And maybe this is not the absolute end of the world.

But as bits of invisible mice go swirling down the drain of my kitchen sink, something is very wrong.

And if we're using Mother Goose metaphors now, then I think it's fair to say that Humpty Dumpty has had a great fall. And all the king's horses and all the king's men need help putting things back together.

And they have no idea where to begin.

Which describes my situation perfectly.

chapter 10

in the air

I'm still sitting at Daddy's desk a few minutes later, and there are footsteps in the walkway, and the door of the study opens.

"Hey, it's me," Bobby says. It's a subdued voice.

Then Gertie trots to my side, licks my hand once, and lies down by the chair.

Bobby says, "She was scratching at the kitchen door, so I let her in. It's getting dark already. Really cold out there."

I nod. "Thanks." I'm quiet a second, and then I ask, "So, you're okay? After helping my dad with that?"

"It was pretty bad," he says, "like, I almost threw up. But I'm okay. I think it was worse for your dad. He actually had names for a lot of the mice. I guess I never thought of a scientist getting attached to lab animals like that."

I nod and say, "I'm not surprised. My dad's the kind of guy who needed a box of tissues when we watched *Bambi* together."

Bobby says, "But it had to be done, I think. Because he's right about trying to control the information. Because that's what we're doing now."

He's next to me now, and the desk creaks as he leans against it.

"Information containment. Damage control," he says. "It's what I've been doing since that very first morning when I couldn't see myself. And I am so sick of it."

It's the tired-little-boy voice again, the one that makes me want to hug him and cradle him in my arms and run my hand through his hair and say, "It's all right, it's all right." But I'm not sure he'd let me do that.

I ask, "Did my dad say anything else about what they've been doing out here?"

"A little," Bobby says. "Because your dad wants us to understand that it's a very big deal, how the two of them have been able to re-create the conditions that trigger the invisibility. Because to do that, they had to work out the science, the principles behind the phenomenon, the precise way that the solar rays interact with the electrical field."

As he talks, the pitch of Bobby's voice rises. This science stuff really gets him going.

"And get this—they've discovered that each time a body goes through a cycle from visible to invisible and back, causing the *next* set of transformations takes *less* energy. So it's like there's a cumulative effect, like the cells are being trained. Some of those mice had been through the complete cycle *five* times."

I nod, pretending I'm more interested in the physics than I really am. And then I ask, "But what about that plan he mentioned, being ready in case the secret gets out—any more about that?"

"Nope," he says. "Nothing. Except that they're not done with the work. Close, but not done. And now he's focused on this immediate situation, and he's really freaked out about the FBI, about maybe having the research stopped. Or stolen."

"And I totally get that," I say.

Bobby says, "Yeah, me too." Then, after a moment, "How about you—are you okay? I can tell you've been crying."

He's next to the desk chair now, and he puts a hand on my shoulder. Such a simple gesture, but it makes my eyes fill up again.

Because I feel like we're traveling through light-years of empty space, trying to get close to each other. And his journey might be just as long and dark as mine. But he's taking risks, coming closer. Close enough to touch me.

I brush my eyes with the back of my hand. "I'm all right. Thanks."

And here we are, just the two of us, alone.

And are we talking about us, about our lives, our futures? And how we feel about each other? No. We're talking about dead mice and global meltdown.

But feelings are in the air. They are. And that moment for ourselves, I'm still hoping we both want it. I'm still hoping it will come.

He takes his hand off my shoulder and says, "Listen, there's a lot going on around here, and I feel like I'm sort of in the way—along with the men William says are following me. So I'm going to drive back home now. I already told your dad. And if anyone wants to follow me, so what? I'm going to go home, and nuke some frozen lasagna, and then practice my trumpet for an hour or two, act like it's an ordinary winter afternoon."

He starts to move away, but stops, turns toward me. I can feel it.

He says, "And maybe when all this calms down, we can get together later tonight. Sound okay to you?"

It doesn't, because I really want him to stay. But I don't want to be clingy, so I say, "Sure, that's fine. And call me, like, if anything happens, okay?"

"Right," he says, "and you keep in touch too. Because I can be back over here in minutes . . . as long as I can get the station wagon started."

I get up, and Gertie comes to heel on my left side. I find her harness handle on Daddy's desk, clip it in place. "I'll walk out with you. I'll have to close the garage door."

"Here," and he takes my right hand and guides it to his left elbow.

And even though I've got Gertie ready, I take his arm. "Thanks."

We don't talk until we're in the garage. Then I say, "So, be careful, all right?"

He says, "You mean, like, be careful that I don't burn

my mouth with hot lasagna? Yeah, I'll be *super* careful. 'Cause that could mess up my trumpet playing for a week."

We both laugh a little, and then we have a quick hug. Hardly a hug at all. But it's something. And feelings are still in the air.

I push the button and the garage door rises.

His car door groans open, and he says, "See you later, okay?"

"Not if I see you first."

And I see his smile as the heavy door slams shut.

The engine starts, the car backs out, and he's gone.

chapter 11

up to a point

Gertie and I make our way back through Daddy's office into the house. And as I cross the little landing toward the kitchen, I can still imagine I hear the garbage disposal running.

But it's not, and Gertie leads me up the four steps into the kitchen. Such a good dog. Girl's best friend.

I can hear Daddy on the phone in the family room. I go out the kitchen door, take a sharp left, and then it's ten steps.

As I'm coming into the room, Daddy's finishing up. ". . . No, that's all right. Can you leave a message for him, please? . . . Yes, tell him that Dr. Van Dorn called, and that our research has hit a snag. . . . No, snag—that's s-n-a-g, snag. . . . Yes, that's right. . . . Thank you. Good-bye."

He hangs up. "Just trying to get in touch with Dr. Phillips. The hotel clerk in Geneva thought I was saying that our research had hit a 'snack.' "

He chuckles, and I'm amazed he's still got his sense of humor.

I'm on the couch now, the faint smell of worn leather around me as I sink into the pillows, and ten feet in front of me I can hear the news. It's CNN, the volume down low, a group of serious people talking about tensions in the Middle East. Daddy can't be in the same room with a TV without lighting it up. And I don't like that, because that always seems like something old people do. And I hate thinking that Daddy is going to get old.

"So," I say, pointing toward the TV, "are we on the news, anything about invisible people? Or mice?"

"Not yet." No smile in his voice.

I shouldn't have said that, and right away I say, "Sorry. That you and Bobby had to do that."

"Yes," he says, "so am I. Brutal, but necessary. 'I was just obeying orders'—isn't that what people always say at moments like this?"

"I really think you had to do it, Daddy. To keep the information secret."

He doesn't respond, and he drops heavily onto the couch at my right. I hear the volume of the news go up a click or two. And I know what's happening. Daddy's dealing with a serious overload, and now he's vegging out, eyes on the screen as there's a bulletin about the closing numbers on the New York Stock Exchange.

"So, what's next?" I ask, because I want to keep him here, keep him engaged. And there's so much more I want to know.

I feel him shrug.

And he says, "I don't know. I guess we have to see what the FBI has to say. See if they're really after our secrets."

"But really," I say, "what *can* they do? It's not like we're criminals. We haven't broken any laws, none of us has. It's not illegal to make a discovery. Or to keep a secret. Companies do that all the time. And so do universities, inventors, lots of people. There's nothing wrong with keeping something a secret."

Gertie stirs at my feet. She doesn't like it when I get emotional.

Daddy says, "You're right about secrets, but only up to a point. When it comes to matters of national security, the government has incredibly broad powers. For example, companies can't sell certain computers to certain countries, because they could be weaponized. It's the same for anything to do with nuclear energy."

It's almost like Daddy's talking to himself, thinking it through.

"Because laws about private property go right out the window when it comes to weapons. And the government would certainly view the ability to make a person invisible as a kind of weapon system. We've still got to keep this away from everybody, and especially the government. Because if the government moves in and declares that this is *their* secret, then there's big trouble. This would be huge, a top-secret, eyes-only, national–security type technology."

Daddy leans forward on the couch, fully back in the here and now, reasoning this out for both of us.

"*Except* the government would have a problem. Because there are at least six other people who know about it, outside people, civilians—us. So they'd have to keep watching all of us, right? Day and night. They'd have to. And when the information leaks out one day—and history proves that it *will* leak out, that there are these six people in Chicago who know how the whole invisibility process works—what then? Then there will be *other* people who will want to talk to us. They will want to *make* us talk to them. And then our government will have to figure out a way to keep us safe from all the others."

Daddy leans back heavily, as though the weight of it all is on his shoulders, then pushes out a long breath.

"And it'll never end, Alicia. It'll never end."

There's a noise from the front of the house, and Gertie tenses, scrambles to her feet—my own personal early-warning system, my secret weapon. I tense too, hold my breath.

Then, from the front hallway, "Hi, I'm home."

It's Mom.

Daddy calls, "We're in here, Julia."

Mom bustles in, kisses Daddy's cheek, then drops onto the couch on my left, leans over, and kisses my cheek too. I feel the cold radiating off her coat.

"You look nice today." Then, without even half a beat, she says, "Could you switch over to channel two,

Leo? They've got a satellite truck at Ellis and University, and I heard sirens a few minutes ago."

A woman's voice comes from the TV. ". . . whether there have been any injuries. But we do know that the library has been completely evacuated. There are police with bomb-sniffing dogs, and you can see that they've already set up barricades on the streets around this part of the campus. Phil? Can you hear me?"

"Yes, Janet. Phil Granby here, and right behind me you can see the main entrance area of the library, and I'm speaking with Officer Susan Wozniak of the University of Chicago security force. Officer Wozniak, what can you tell us about the situation?"

"At approximately three-fifteen this afternoon, the library received a phone call stating there was a bomb inside. Security officers began evacuating the building immediately, and also contacted the Chicago police. Now the police and the FBI are on the scene, and the building is being searched. There have been no injuries, and all students and staff have safely exited the building."

"Hey—Alicia . . . ease up."

And Daddy taps my hand. With good reason. I've got a killer grip on his forearm. Instinct. Tensed up by this news. Because the FBI isn't looking for a bomb with those dogs. I don't believe that for a second.

And out loud I say, "They're looking for William."

"For whom?" Mom asks. Perfect grammar.

Daddy says, "A man Bobby found in New York. He's invisible."

And I'm stunned by how casually Daddy says it—"He's invisible," just like that. It's not new to him at all, not odd, not weird. Just one more scientific fact.

Daddy's still talking, bringing Mom up to date. And when he tells her that Bobby was here earlier, she interrupts, almost as if the news about William was nothing, and she turns to me and says, "I'm glad Bobby's back—I know you've been missing him." And she pats my knee.

And again, I'm sort of stunned, because Mom never seems to want me to have anything to do with Bobby.

Daddy finishes the narrative, and when he's done, she says, "But if they're really after this William fellow now, how did they know to look for him there at the library?" she asks.

A sinking feeling, and I put it into words. "Because of me. People were watching Bobby, and then he and I were together at the library, so someone began watching me. And I was sitting near the entrance when William came up to me. Someone must have seen me talking . . . to no one."

Daddy says, "It's not your fault, Alicia."

Gertie leans against my legs and gives a low whine, almost a yawning sound. And she bumps me twice.

I know what she needs, and I stand up. "Gertie's got to go out."

Mom and Dad don't seem to hear because the woman reporter is talking, this time to a university official, and Mom says, "Look—that's Carla Untermeyer."

I follow Gertie to the kitchen, down the four steps, and she's at the back door, her nose just below the knob to help me locate it. Such a sweet dog.

As I pat her back, she sniffs the door. And she freezes, the hair on her shoulders suddenly stiff and bristly. And she growls.

She never does that.

And through the glass, a voice, soft. A person in distress. An Englishman.

"Please, Alicia, I need to get indoors."

Sirens go off inside my head, alarm bells too. Nothing subtle about the desperation in the man's voice, not now. It's right at the surface. He's a drowning man with one hand on the side of a canoe. My canoe.

And I want to turn around, run up the back staircase to the bathroom, shut and lock the door, slip into a hot bath, put on my headphones, listen to a long novel, listen to poetry, listen to Mozart and Miles Davis. Until all this goes away.

But I can't do that. I can't run from this.

And despite my fears, I know Gertie will protect me. And the man has to be freezing to death out there.

So I hold my dog's harness, and I say, "Gertie, hush. *Hush.*"

And I open the door.

chapter 12
felonies

"Th-thank you. It's . . . so . . . cold."

The man whispers, teeth chattering as we stand on the landing inside the back door.

"Down here," and I reach for the basement door.

With the door open, a big breath of warm air rises and surrounds us. The furnace in this old house is huge.

"You first." I flip the light switch on my right. The treads creak as he walks down, and I follow with Gertie, pulling the door shut behind us, my right hand on the smooth wooden handrail. It's six steps down to the concrete floor. "Should be socks and some other clothes on the wooden rack by the washer."

"Yes. Wonderful. Do you think anyone will mind?"

I push my fears aside, try to sound as if it's normal to be helping an invisible man get dressed right in front of me. "No, not at all."

Gertie growls, then almost yips, and I know if she

starts barking, Mom and Dad will hear. "Gertie, *hush!* Good girl."

And I make a show of having to restrain her. I want this man to know that she's my protector. And my family's protector. Bobby's too.

I put a hard edge on my voice, a take-charge tone.

"You need to stay put down here, and you have to keep quiet. Because you were right about Bobby being followed. And me too. It's the FBI."

And I'm pleased at how I sound, very no-nonsense, strong.

But then I can't help asking, "Will you be all right?"

"I think so," he says, "yes. Thanks so much. I just need to warm up."

His words are strained, the voice of someone in pain.

Then he says, "Is Bobby here? Because I really need to talk to him. . . . I think he's still in more danger than he knows."

I want to ask what he means by that, but I don't want the power to shift, don't want to make William feel like he's in charge. Because he isn't.

That's what I tell myself.

I put on my strong voice again. "He's not here, but he might come back later on." Because that's what I hope.

"Well," he says, "tell him I must speak with him, all right? Please?"

I nod, and say, "I will." But only because he said "please."

And our conversation is over.

Gertie and I are up the stairs with the door open, and now on the landing, and I step aside and close the basement door.

And I turn the dead bolt. I'm locking him down there. And I wish this door had another lock. Or two.

I stand still for almost a minute, my back against the locked door, until my breathing is almost back to normal.

As I start up the stairs, I can tell Gertie wants to stay on the landing and be a watchdog. I'm halfway through the kitchen before she scrambles up the steps and comes with me toward the family room.

And as I turn left out of the kitchen doorway, I'm already framing an announcement to my parents, imagining how to break this news story.

Maybe, "Guess who I've got locked in the basement?"

Or, "I know for a fact that the police are *not* going to find anyone at the library."

The local news is still on the TV, and I'm four steps from the family room door when Gertie doubles back past me and trots along the front hallway. And two seconds later the doorbell rings.

The TV goes mute, and Daddy says, "Damn it!—I should have been out back erasing my files. That has to be the FBI."

Daddy almost never swears.

Mom hurries out of the family room, and as she passes me, she says, "I'll get the door, Alicia. Your father thinks it's going to be the FBI."

Makes sense to me. The agent said he needed to talk to all three of us. If they're watching the house, they'll know Mom and Dad are home now.

Or . . . did they follow William here?

And that thought snaps a jolt of fear through me, makes my breathing go all ragged again.

Over her shoulder, Mom says, "And if it is the FBI, then we just say as little as possible, all right?"

I'm surprised that Mom's being so steady, so unemotional about this. And it's not an act. She's actually calm. Plus, a little earlier, she made a genuinely friendly comment about Bobby.

It's an odd moment to be making realizations, standing here with my heart pounding away, but it strikes me that I haven't been letting Mom grow much, letting my view of her change. I've been so busy fighting my own battles that I haven't noticed she's been winning some too.

I hear Mom open the front door, and then a male voice.

Then, "Alicia? Leo? Would you come to the parlor? We have guests."

Mom's using her hostess voice.

Daddy comes out of the family room and offers me his arm. He whispers, "Let's keep this real simple, okay? Don't volunteer any information."

When we're in the doorway, Mom takes charge. "Alicia, there's room over here on the couch. Leo, this is Agent Porter of the New York bureau of the FBI—did I get that right?"

"Yes, ma'am. Special Agent Charles Porter."

"And this is Agent Joan Argus. And they'd like to ask us some questions, right?"

The man says, "That's right. We're here because an acquaintance of your daughter's, Robert Phillips, had contact with a man known as William. We believe these two first met in New York City and that they had some kind of disagreement there. And we think this man may have followed Robert here to Chicago. The man is wanted in New York for questioning and for resisting arrest, and we think he may be a danger to Mr. Phillips, and possibly to his friends and acquaintances. So first, I'd like to know if any of you have seen Robert Phillips in the past eight hours."

Without a trace of hesitation, my mom says, "He was here visiting my daughter less than an hour ago. And Alicia saw him earlier at the library too. They've been close friends for a long time. And since his parents are away until Sunday, we're sort of watching out for him until they get back. He may come back and join us for supper in a little while."

So Mom knows that Bobby's parents are away. Makes sense, since they've all been in cahoots about the research.

I'm smiling and nodding, totally blown away by

Mom's coolness, and that bit about supper was a nice touch.

And I see how this conversation is going to go. That first question was a test, because the agents already knew the answer. They've been following Bobby, so they must have seen him come here and then drive away again—*unless* . . . unless the people following Bobby aren't with the FBI at all.

I wish Bobby hadn't left. I mean, I know I can get along fine on my own, I'm sure of that. But I don't *want* to be on my own. And I want to know that Bobby's safe. And close.

My dad says, "This man, William—you don't have his whole name?"

"No," Agent Porter says. "He's been . . . difficult to identify."

"Can you show us a photo so we can watch out for him?" Daddy says.

Brilliant question. Because it's impossible for them to have a photo. But the question tells them that *we* think William is just a normal guy. I'm surrounded by smart people here.

The other agent, the woman, clears her throat. "We've only got a physical description. He's a white male, age thirty-five to forty, about five feet, eight inches tall, shoulder-length hair, wiry build, and he speaks with a British accent."

Daddy says, "Even around the university, there aren't many men that age with shoulder-length hair, so someone like that would stand out, accent or not. But, of course, he could easily change his hair."

"Right," says the woman. "So, you or your wife, you haven't seen him . . . or spoken with him?"

Mom says, "No, I'm sure I haven't. Have you, Leo?"

"No. I'm certain of it."

Agent Porter says, "How about you, Alicia? A university security guard thinks he saw you talking to someone at the library earlier this afternoon."

And just like that, I'm on the spot.

I want to tell the truth. Because sooner or later, reality occurs.

But I'm more scared about our secret getting out than I am about lying.

So I give a sheepish smile and say, "Someone could have seen me talking to my dog. I do that a lot. And I talk to myself too. Which I know is weird. But, like, is that why you followed me home from the library? Because some guard said I might have talked to someone?"

The woman clears her throat, then rustles some paper, and I can picture her flipping the pages of a small black notebook, checking her facts. And ready to write down every word I say.

She says, "We're just checking out all the links to the suspect, miss. And Robert Phillips is our best link to the man at the moment. And you're linked to him."

She's got a pleasant voice, no particular accent. A reasonable voice. Like my history teacher.

"And this man," I ask, "is he dangerous? Like, does he have a criminal record and everything? Fingerprints and all that?"

More paper rustling, and the sound of a ballpoint pen scratching away. "We're not permitted to discuss details of an ongoing investigation," she says. "All I can tell you is that he's wanted for resisting arrest in New York City."

I smile in her direction, but I keep drilling in. "And the FBI got involved because he resisted arrest? Or is he wanted for a lot of other crimes too?" I'm pushing it now, but these questions are important. If this William is a serious criminal, I need to know that right now.

Agent Porter says, "When a fugitive crosses state lines, then it becomes a federal matter. Like Agent Argus said, we can't discuss details. But it's important that if you have any contact at all with this man, you give us a call right away, okay?"

I nod, and say, "Sure." Which is a lie.

Both agents stand up, and so do my mom and dad. I stay on the couch, scratching behind Gertie's ears.

Agent Porter says, "Thanks for taking the time to talk with us." As he talks, his voice moves toward the front hall, then stops. More rustling, this time into a pocket, or maybe a briefcase.

"Here's my card, and this is the number where you can reach us. And one last thing. We think this man is extremely . . . clever. Please don't get tricked into helping him. Anyone who knowingly assists this man or fails to report any information they may have about him is committing a federal offense—aiding a fugitive from justice, which is a felony. And I wouldn't want you good people to get in trouble on his account."

Daddy's already in the vestibule, and I hear him open the front door. "We'll be careful," he says. "And let us know if there's anything else we can do."

The door closes, and they're gone. But they've left behind a new kind of fear. I've never been a felon before.

Mom sits back down on the couch, pats me on the knee, and says, "Well. That wasn't so bad, was it? Those two seem like very decent people. And you did the right thing, not telling them about talking to that man at the library."

She's still being calm, but she's sounding a little like the old Mom, trying to put a sweetsy spin on a bad situation. Because I've lost count of how many times I'm already guilty of federal crimes.

Daddy's back in the room, and he says, "And how about the way they talk about William, as if he's just another guy who came here from New York? Of course, they have to act that way. As if he's normal. So we have to act that way too. It's important we don't give them any way at all to establish a link between us and William—or his condition. They'd be in here with a warrant in no time. Even if they do end up catching him, as long as there's no provable connection to us, we'll still be all right. And they won't be able to prove anything that

William might tell them about Bobby. It'll be Bobby's word against his. Still, the best would be if William were to simply disappear again."

Gertie pulls away and I hear her claws click on the hardwood in the corner of the parlor. She growls, and then scratches at the metal floor grate.

It's William's scent, drifting up through the heating vent. He's probably been right below us, listening to all of this.

"Gertie, here." She comes back and sits in front of me.

Daddy says, "What's bothering her?"

I shrug. "Too many strangers, I guess."

And this sick feeling grabs at my stomach.

Because I've just told Daddy a lie.

And I feel like I don't quite know him anymore, this dad who zaps mice into transparency and then grinds them up at the kitchen sink. He feels bad about it, but, still, is this the same Daddy who used to read *The Wind in the Willows* to me?

And I've got this mom now who's suddenly behaving like a real human being, like a person I could talk to, except I don't dare. And she just told me I did the right thing by lying.

Mom says, "Everything okay, Alicia?"

She's worried—I must look awful.

I throw a quick smile onto my face.

"Yeah, I'm fine."

Another lie.

Mom shifts gears and says, "So, is everybody hungry? How about we order in Chinese—sound good? Alicia, why don't you give Bobby a call and tell him he's invited—I wasn't just saying that. And while we're waiting we can have some cheese and crackers, maybe some fruit?"

Daddy says, "Sounds great. I'm famished."

And the two of them are headed for the kitchen. How can they think about food—especially Daddy?

Over her shoulder, Mom calls, "Alicia, come help out, okay?"

I can hear the tinge of forced cheeriness in her voice, and that's for me, and for Daddy too. Because she's trying to keep a grip on normal life. Both of them are. And I don't blame them for wanting that. Not at all.

And they vanish toward the kitchen in a fading cloud of small talk. As if all our problems are over now.

A sudden rush of gratitude seizes me, forces a lump into my throat. Because Mom and Dad have always tried so hard to keep me safe, to keep me happy, to keep me from making terrible mistakes. And my teeth clamp together, my jaw muscles tighten from the fierceness of my love for these two people. What I want most is to make sure they do not have to endure one more heartache because of me. Not one more.

And that feels so impossible.

Mom calls again, "Alicia?"

I call back, "In a minute."

I'm alone in the dark.

And I feel William, sitting somewhere below the floor, like a time bomb that could blow up my home, lift my whole life right off its foundation. And I feel those agents outside, close by, secure within the power of the law, watching, biding their time as the dim afternoon light fades away. And Bobby, who's home from New York now, but still so far away.

"Gertie, here."

And she comes and puts her head on my knees.

She knows I'm shaky.

"Good girl, good girl." I lean forward and hug her, and I fight not to burst into tears. I fight hard.

Because I'm not doing that. I'm not going to fall apart. I'm not.

No matter how surreal things get, I'm still me. I know that. Who I am and what I am does not change, does not disappear, does not fade away.

I know that. I've had to *prove* that.

I'm Alicia. It's me.

Yes, I broke the law when I let that man into the basement. And, yes, I broke the law again when I didn't open up to the FBI agent.

And I don't think the agent believed me, about not talking to anyone at the library. He was hoping I'd be more afraid.

And William? He wants me to be afraid too, afraid of the FBI, afraid for Bobby.

Even my own parents want me to be afraid so I won't talk, won't ask too many questions, won't rock the boat. They want me to sit quietly.

In the dark. Alone.

No, that's not true. They'd help if they could. Because Mom and Dad don't know the whole situation.

Neither does Bobby.

But I did not invite this stuff into my life. It's not my fault, none of it.

And I'm afraid.

There. I said it: I'm afraid.

Honesty.

I stare into the darkness, and I hold on to Gertie, and I remember about honesty.

Because, above all, blindness has forced me to be honest.

And forced me to be humble enough to ask for help.

Because asking for help is not weakness.

It takes courage. And faith.

Sometimes it even takes love. And trust.

And right now, tonight? This is one of those times.

chapter 13

we

obby wasn't kidding about how fast he could get back over here. I called him seven or eight minutes ago, caught him with a mouth full of lasagna. But it was only his first bite, so he stuck the rest in the fridge, hopped in the car, and now he's in our kitchen. Again.

And I'm glad he wanted to come.

Daddy's been telling Bobby about the visit from the FBI, but I can tell no one else wants to think about all that right now. Mom changes the subject.

"So, how did your auditions go, Bobby?" she says. "Was it four or five that you took?"

"Five," he says, "and I think most of them went pretty well. The best was my jazz audition at this school in New Jersey, William Paterson."

"So," she asks, "is that one you'd like to go to, if you get accepted?"

"Still not sure," he says.

"Well, all those eastern schools are so good. I'm sure you'll find the one that's just right."

And I've got this sudden feeling that Mom is being nice to Bobby because she's sure he's going to be completely out of my life by the end of August.

Except I'm not letting that happen.

Daddy says, "Alicia, the food should be here any minute. So here's the money, two twenties. Ask for four dollars in change, okay? That'll still leave a nice tip for the driver."

Daddy's always doing stuff like this, making me handle cash, making me pump gas at the self-serve island, making me check in the luggage when we go to the airport. He tells me what to do and then walks away. And it's good. Independence training.

"Right," I say, and I'm on my feet. He hands me the bills and I start for the front hallway. And I say, "Bobby, want to help me carry the food?"

"Sure," he says.

But I don't need help carrying the food. I need other help.

Two years ago Bobby was alone, lost, out in the cold. Until he trusted me.

And now the wheel has come full circle.

We're in the front parlor and he's chewing. "Want a grape?"

Then he's in front of me and he sees my face.

"What? What is it?"

I put a finger to my lips, and I whisper, "Bobby, I did a stupid thing."

I take his arm and pull him to the opposite corner of the room, away from the iron floor grate that opens into the basement.

"I let William into the house, here, just a few minutes before the FBI came. He's locked down in the basement. He was freezing, and I let him in. I had to."

It takes a second for that to sink in.

He whispers too. "So . . . William got himself out of the library . . . and he came here?"

I nod. "And I know I shouldn't have let him in. But I had to."

He's quiet for five or ten seconds, and I'm so afraid he's going to tell me what an idiot I am.

Then he asks, "How did he know where you live?"

I shrug, surprised by the question. "I guess he looked up the address. He knew my last name."

"You told him your whole name?" he whispers.

I shake my head. "No, he already knew it when he first talked to me at the library. He must have heard you say my name to Gwen. In New York."

"Uh-uh, no way," he says. "I told Gwen about *Alicia*. That's all I ever said to her. Alicia. I'm sure of it."

"And what did you say?"

"What . . . ?"

"About Alicia. To Gwen." I'm swerving off course. But I need to hear this.

Bobby's still whispering, and I can hear a half smile in his voice. "That she's pretty. And brave. And smart."

I love hearing him say that, but I snort. "Right, real smart. Lets some creep she knows nothing about right into her house. Brilliant."

Bobby's back on the problem. "So . . . William knew your last name. And he came to your house. And you let him in."

I nod. "And now I've given the police everything they need to put all of us in jail, and sweep in here and seize all our dads' research, everything."

Bobby takes my right hand. Long cool fingers. A gentle squeeze.

"That's not gonna happen. This whole thing stinks."

"I know, Bobby, and I'm so sorry I got us into this mess, really," and I feel like I'm going to choke up.

"No," he whispers quickly, "I mean it stinks like entrapment, like a setup. It has to be. William shows up at the university library, and he knows your whole name. Then they stage a bomb scare and pretend to hunt for him, which gives him an excuse to come here. Right where they want him. You let him in, and now it looks like we're hiding a fugitive, like we're all breaking the law. So we feel like we have to cooperate or get arrested. I don't think William's a fugitive. I think he's been forced to become a federal employee. He's working for the FBI now—nothing else makes sense. They're using him to get to the information, the whole secret, the process. So it's not your fault. I think you were set up."

"But even if all that's true," I say, "if I hadn't let him *in*, we wouldn't be stuck like this."

He pulls me closer, one arm around my back, and he says, "Listen, it'll be okay. They say the food in jail isn't so bad, once you get used to it."

A little laugh from both of us.

And we hug. A long hug, and he drops his head and puts his face into the hollow of my shoulder, against my neck, and I feel him draw in a long breath through his nose. He's inhaling me. And I'm melting.

And as I melt, I'm mapping this scene in my mind, the parlor, where we're standing, how we're making one shadow on the wall, the texture of the carpet under our feet, because I want to be able to see this again, to feel it right here in my heart anytime I—

"Alicia?"

Mom, calling from the kitchen. The woman has boy radar.

I take a half step back, and I call, "What, Mom?"

"Ask for extra soy sauce, okay? The driver will probably have some with him."

"Okay," I yell back.

So our hugging scene is over. But not erased, not deleted. It's on pause.

Whispering again, I ask Bobby, "So, any ideas about William? What we should do?"

"Actual ideas? No, not really. But for starters, we'll

eat some food. And we'll think. Maybe invite William upstairs to have some pork fried rice? Probably not. I'm not sure what we should do. But I know we can figure it out. I'm sure we can."

And I love that word. We.

Gertie whines, feeling left out, and I reach down and pat her head. "Good girl." Because I need her help too. We all need each other.

The doorbell rings, and I deal with the transaction. And I remember to get some extra soy sauce.

I've got a grip on one bag, and Bobby's carrying two, and the food smells great, and all of a sudden I'm starving.

"Let's go," Bobby says, and he guides my hand to his elbow.

And we head for the kitchen—boy, girl, dog.

And I feel so much better. About everything. For the moment.

chapter 14

quiz show

Robert! I am so glad to see you."

"You don't have to whisper," Bobby says. "Alicia's parents just went out to buy some ice cream. Here's some food."

It's Bobby, Gertie, and me in the basement. With William.

And what Bobby said is true. My folks are getting some ice cream. After dinner Daddy said, "We want to look as normal as possible, and if this were a normal situation, my wife and I would go bring home some fantastic ice cream for dessert." And they both got in the Saab and left.

But I wouldn't be surprised if Daddy picked up his lab notes and a portable hard drive on the way to the garage through his study. And those files could already be tucked away for safekeeping somewhere between here and Steve's Ice Cream Shop.

That's what I would have done. In a situation like this.

I hate it that I have to think like this. And I also hate that I'm so good at it.

We've got about fifteen minutes before my mom and dad get back, and we're going at the William problem straight on. And we have a script.

Bobby starts it off. "So let's hear it, William—why are you here?"

William already has a mouthful of General Tso's chicken. "I came here because *you* weren't home. I went to your house first, and there was no one there. And I deduced that you'd be at your girlfriend's. So I came here. With all possible haste. Feels as if I almost lost some toes from the cold."

I've got my back against one of the thick square wooden posts that hold up the house, and it's my line next. "How did you know where I lived, William?"

"I looked it up in the phone book. There are only three Van Dorns in all of Chicago, and only one is within walking distance of campus. I checked the locations with Google Maps at an open computer terminal."

Bobby says, "But I never told you Alicia's last name, William. Ever."

"You didn't have to tell me. Earlier today I followed the men who were following you when you and Alicia went to that study room on the third floor of the library. And after the men looked at the sign-up sheet at the information desk by the third-floor elevators, I looked at it too, and there it was in black and white: Van Dorn, comma, Alicia. First and last names. Signed up for room 307. Why are you quizzing me like this?"

Bobby's voice is hard, accusing. "You've got ears. You heard the FBI agents when they were here, right? You probably listened at a heat vent, heard everything they said. Did you hear Alicia lie about talking to you? And now you're hiding here in the Van Dorns' house. So that means she broke the law, and now we're all harboring a fugitive. And any minute, the FBI is going to show up with a search warrant. And arrest warrants too. Is that how it's going to be?"

"You . . . you think I'm working for *them*?" he says. "Of all the *bloody* fool things—why would I do that? I've no reason to help them. They want to put me in jail, plus do God-knows-what-else to me. I am trying to do *one* thing, and one thing only: I want to get my life back. And I'm sorry I tried to bully you into helping me in New York. But I still believe you can help me, and I've come halfway across America in that hope. I am *begging* for your help. If you have any idea about how to help me, for the love of God, please tell me. And if you can swear, right now, that you *cannot* help me, then I'll gladly leave. I shall walk out into the night this instant. No one will ever know I've spoken to either of you. And the police and the FBI will never find me again. No one will."

Gertie doesn't like emotional outbursts. She comes to her feet and leans against my leg.

"Gertie, sit. Good girl." And facing William, I say, "So you didn't lead the FBI here?"

"*Think*, Alicia! If the scenario you two have imagined were correct, they'd have come blazing into this home an hour ago. The FBI came here because they are doing efficient police work. They're after me, but they're following *Robert*. I'm certain of it."

"Well, I'm not," Bobby says. "Enjoy the food. And don't make a mess. And be ready to hide if anyone else comes down here. We'll let you know what happens next."

Bobby sounds so strong, confident—as if we really know what happens next.

But as we head back up the basement steps, I'm pretty sure that neither one of us has a clue.

chapter 15

trust

We go up the basement steps to the landing, and I hear Bobby lock the basement door. "Family room?" I ask.

He says, "Sure," and once we're there, Bobby puts on a jazz CD, then sits beside me on the couch. He pushes the volume up and leans toward me, talking in my ear. "So he can't hear us talking."

The precaution seems a little silly. But after a visit from the FBI, I guess it's not.

Again, close to my ear. "What do you think?"

He turns his head, and I say, "I believe him. I think we should help him."

"Really?" he says. "How come?"

It takes a moment to compose my thoughts. "Well . . . ," I say, "when he was talking, down in the basement? I thought I'd never heard anyone sound so desperate. But that's not true. Because I heard you talking the same way, two years ago. And I've felt that way too. I don't think a person can fake that. Do you?"

He's quiet a second. And I wish I could see his face.

But I can picture Bobby's eyebrows bunched up like they do when he's thinking. Or angry. Or both. I've touched those eyebrows.

And I know his lips are pressed together in a tight line. I've touched his lips too.

Ahem—Buttercup? Oh, Buttercup? It's the Brain Fairy. Can you hear me? I can't see you. There seems to be this soft, pink haze, sort of like lots of little bunnies made of cotton candy, and they're in my eyes, and they're clogging up my brain. No—wait, they're clogging your *brain!*

Listen, just because *you* don't seem to have a heart doesn't mean *I* can't have one. So butt out.

I'm just saying that this is a time for thinking, not feeling. That's all.

Listen, I *like* feeling this way about Bobby. And there's nothing wrong with that.

True. But do you have to get moony about every little thing? You're in the middle of a hazardous situation. Clarity, Buttercup. Clarity is crucial.

Mind your own business, all right? And don't call me Buttercup.

You are *my business. Buttercup.*

Bobby's been thinking during my private conversation, and now he leans near again. "Just because William is genuinely desperate doesn't mean he's being honest. I still don't trust the guy. I mean, for all we know, he's got a little transmitter hidden in the palm of his hand, and he's relaying everything he hears to the FBI. If we keep helping him, we're just getting in deeper and deeper."

I'm not sure how to respond. And I'm not sure I'm right, not completely. And I don't want to have an argument about this. Still, as I listened to William talking earlier, I think I saw something true, just for a second. And even a glimpse of truth can't be ignored.

"But William doesn't trust the FBI, Bobby," I whisper, "or the police. He trusts us. He's putting all his faith in you and me. And I heard that when he talked to us."

Bobby doesn't answer, but the tone of the silence tells me he's not convinced.

I lean closer, my forehead right above his ear, touching. There's a slight scent of citrus in his hair, a hint of cologne rising from his neck. And I whisper, "Bobby, I know you remember how it feels to be that way, to have so little hope that things can ever get back to normal. To feel completely dependent on others, to feel caught by forces beyond your control, to feel alone, to feel . . ."

My voice wavers, and I have to stop. Because . . . because I'm not talking about William anymore. I'm talking about myself.

I feel Bobby nod his head. And he whispers, "I see what you mean. And you're right, especially about that feeling. Feeling like things will never get back to normal."

The whispering keeps us close, shoulders angled, almost face-to-face.

He leans closer, his lips almost brushing my ear. "And, really, Alicia . . . I don't know how you do it. With the blindness. Every day. It's not a small thing."

I love this moment. I love it way too much. And I have to gulp back a wave of emotion. Then I say, "Thanks—that means a lot, Bobby." And before I slip into even deeper waters, I straighten up, push my back into the leather cushions of the couch. And I say, "So, do you think what our dads have been doing can help him?"

"What do you mean?" And his tone is instantly sharp and analytical.

Bobby amazes me, how he can flip a switch and be 110 percent business again. So I have to go right along with him.

I say, "Our dads have been experimenting, right? And if you have the equipment that can make someone invisible, then you can use the same stuff to reverse the process. Right?"

He says, "Well, we know that they had to generate an electrical force field, put the subject in it, and then bombard the field and the subject with the same type of energy stream that gets released by a solar flare. And we also know that they've figured out the principles, and then they actually did a series of successful lab tests.

But they've been working with *mice*, Alicia. A mouse weighs only about twenty grams. And that means the scale they've been working at is way too small, probably by some factor of ten. So, bottom line? I don't think your father's little backyard lab is ready to readjust the molecular light-reflecting properties of a full-grown man."

It's quiet a moment, and I hear the blower of our old furnace kick on, feel the warm air start to circulate from the floor grate across the room.

Bobby gives a short laugh, then says, "And if your dad knew this guy was in his basement, endangering you this way, *plus* putting the secret at risk—would your dad want to *help* him . . . or would the professor want to take some *other* course of action? Good question, huh? Let's just say that if Dr. Leo knew, I would *not* like to be in William's shoes."

"What do you mean by that?" I snap. "Are you saying my dad would do something to harm him, do something . . . bad? He would *never* do that."

"To protect you and your mom?" Bobby asks. "Think again. All I know is, those mice didn't last long, did they?"

"But that was different. It was." And I have to stop talking, stop thinking about this. Because, honestly, I don't know what Daddy would do. If he knew where William was right now.

Bobby sits beside me, and the sound of a jazz trumpet fills the room.

And he just sits, breathing in and out, long, deep breaths.

Again, I wish I could see his face.

I nudge him and whisper, "What?"

He says, "I think I should get William out of here, right now, take him to my house. Once I get him out to my car, if we got caught, none of you would be in trouble. Like William said, the FBI is following *me*. None of this would be happening if I hadn't messed up *first*. And I can get him out of here before your mom and dad come back."

So sweet. He's trying to take this whole problem onto himself. To keep me safe—me and my parents, I mean. So *sweet*. Makes me want to hug him and never let go.

Oh, Buttercup . . . I see the pink bunnies. . . .

I reach for his hand anyway.

And I whisper, "You can't do that, Bobby. And anyway, I don't think William would go with you."

"Yeah he would. If he's as desperate as we both think he is, he'd do anything I tell him to. He believes I can help him. He trusts us, remember? And the sad truth is I can't help him, not really. And I'm not sure anyone can, not even our dads. There's no way they can help William, at least not anytime soon."

He trails off into another long pause. This time

there's a bass solo filling the air. When we came into this room, he didn't flip any light switches. So it's dim in here, dim and bluesy.

I squeeze his hand, and I say, "Bobby?"

"What?"

"If I tell you something, you promise you won't get mad at me, no matter what?"

He laughs a little, and says, "Logically, that's an impossible promise to make."

"Then stop being logical," I say. "I'm serious."

"Then I promise." And he's serious too.

I take a deep breath. "I think there's a way we can help William."

"You mean, like, you and me?" Bobby whispers. "How?"

It takes me a long time, but I finally say, "Remember Sheila?"

"Yeah," he says, "of course I do."

And I know he remembers, because Sheila made a huge difference in the way things turned out for Bobby. We found Sheila two years ago, when Bobby was invisible. She was like William—the invisibility seemed to hit her out of nowhere, and she'd decided to use it, to embrace it. She used it to run away from her old life. And us finding Sheila, talking to her, comparing experiences, that was a big part of what helped us figure out the problem for Bobby back then. And after his own readjustment worked, Bobby told her about it, offered to help her. Except Sheila didn't want to come back. She couldn't face . . . reality. I think about Sheila a lot.

Bobby prompts me, "What about her?"

"About two weeks after you got back to normal, I got a phone call from her."

"From Sheila?" he says. "No way!"

I keep talking fast—it's easier that way. "You'd put my name and phone number in the note, the one you put in the box of things you sent her. So she called me. And she said she didn't want the stuff, said she was never going to want it, said she never wanted to have a visible body again. Said she liked being free. That's what she called it, 'being free.' She was mostly yelling, so angry. And after a few minutes of that, she made me promise I'd never tell another soul about her, told me that if I did, she'd hunt me down and make me sorry I had. So, of course, I promised her, and she slammed the phone down, and that was it. I never told you, Bobby."

"That's *wild*!" he says. "Sheila—I mean, she sounded crazy when I talked to her, but *this* . . . and it's okay you didn't tell me about it. Still . . . I think it would have been all right if you had."

I nod and whisper, "I know, and I'm sorry, Bobby. But there's more. Because three weeks later, I was here at home by myself, and UPS brought a package addressed to me. I opened it, and right away I could tell what it was—the same box of stuff you sent to Sheila. All of it. And I never told you about this either—I just wanted the whole thing to go away."

He's sitting straight up on the couch now. "Alicia, you . . . you still have it? The box?"

"Shh!" I whisper. "William might hear you—and let go."

He's almost breaking my hand, squeezing it hard, freaking out. Because the box he sent to Sheila had an electric blanket in it, an old Sears model with a broken heat controller that sends the wrong kind of power into the blanket's coils. And if the solar winds are blowing, shooting energy into Earth's atmosphere, the malfunctioning blanket creates an electrical energy field that's big enough and powerful enough to affect a full-grown person—a man like William, or a teenager like Bobby, or a woman like Sheila. Because that's what happened to each of them, on different dates, in different places, but each one lying asleep under the same kind of blanket.

Bobby repeats, "You still have the box?"

He puts his ear close to my face again, and I whisper, "I almost trashed everything—didn't want my dad to find the blanket or any of their notes and sketches, didn't want him to start messing around with the physics again. Which is almost more irony than I can stand. And I came close to destroying all of it. But back then I thought, 'What if Sheila changes her mind one day?' So I hid the box away, up in the attic. Everything. Which is another reason to worry about the FBI coming in here with a search warrant."

He's silent, and I don't know what he's thinking. I whisper, "So . . . Bobby, are you angry, that I didn't tell you sooner, like, right after she sent the box to me? Because really, all of that belongs to you."

"No, I'm not mad, not at all. You did the right thing. And this is great news, or it could be."

I whisper, "So . . . you think everything would still work, to do the reversal?"

"Only one way to find out."

I'm finding it hard to whisper. "Then let's grab the box, get William, and go! We can go to your house, right now, like before my parents get back. Because I don't want them to know he was ever here—that way, if things go wrong, they're innocent. And if we can bring William back to normal, that's *huge*! It's like making all the evidence disappear . . . or reappear. Right? So let's go, Bobby!"

He hesitates, then says, "How about this: I take the blanket and I leave with William, right now. And you stay here, Alicia. Because I really don't want you to be on the hook for William. Like I said, this all started with me getting the police involved. So let me be the one to get him away from here for you, okay?"

So sweet. And unselfish. And I want to hug him and say, "Bobby, don't you *get* it? If it's *your* problem, it's *my* problem too." Except then I'd get another visit from the Brain Fairy, telling me that my feelings are getting too warm and fuzzy.

But that *is* how I feel. I want us to do this together. Like at the very beginning.

So I shake my head and I say, "No. I'm in this too, all the way. So let's get moving."

And he says, "Okay. But if your dad kills me, it's gonna be your fault."

I was ready for more of a fight. Which means that Bobby really wants my help. He doesn't want to do this all on his own.

Which should not be a surprise, not to me. Because no one wants to be alone. Including William. And even Sheila. Because alone is not the same as free.

I'm on my feet. "Gertie, come."

And we're in motion, because my parents are on their way back home by now. With ice cream. Too bad about that.

But we'll be gone, out into the winter twilight— William, Bobby, Gertie, and me.

And a pink bunny or two.

chapter 16

plan in motion

oesn't this beastly car have a heater?"

William's in the backseat, and I feel sorry for him. Nakedness and frozen leather upholstery has to be a bad combination.

Bobby says, "Takes ten minutes to warm up. And we'll be at my house in five. So just tough it out. And keep your head down."

"Perhaps you'll recall that I'm invisible?" William says.

"Yeah, but your breath isn't. Water vapor plus cold air equals visible clouds. Physics. It's all about the physics."

I ask, "Are we being followed?"

I'm here beside Bobby with my teeth chattering as the old Volvo lurches from stoplight to stoplight, and I've got a box of potentially incriminating information sitting between my feet, and there's an invisible man who's wanted by the FBI making wisecracks from the backseat. So I'm feeling a little exposed.

Bobby says, "I don't know. I'm not even looking at my mirrors. If someone's watching us, I want to look like I don't have a care in the world. I'm just taking my girlfriend out for a drive. Over to my house. And my parents are away."

"Which makes me the chaperone," says William. "How charming."

Bobby used the g-word—he said "my girlfriend." And I wonder if the way he's using that word is changing.

Gertie shifts her weight. She's sitting between Bobby and me on the front seat. She's getting more used to William, hasn't growled at him once since we got in the car. But I can feel her head swing back to look for him every five or ten seconds. And she's sniffing at him like crazy.

I don't know what Bobby told William about why we're taking him to the Phillips's house. After Bobby got the box from the place I'd hidden it in the attic, he carried it out to the car. I had my coat by then, and we met at the basement door. Then he ducked down the steps, and thirty seconds later the three of us hurried through Daddy's study on our way to the garage—four of us, counting Gertie—and William seemed eager to be leaving, eager about everything. Except about the cold.

Dash, dash—vibrations. It's my phone.

Dash, dash.

I have a love/hate relationship with my cell phone. At the moment, it's hate. Because those vibrations are Morse code for the letter *M*, which stands for "Mom."

Which means she got home ten seconds ago, figured out I'm gone, and now she expects a full report.

"Hi, Mom."

"Where are you? I thought we were all going to have ice cream together."

"Yeah, but we decided we wanted hot cocoa instead. And Bobby remembered he has to stop in at home to get a phone call from his parents around seven o'clock. So first we're going to the Starbucks on Fifty-seventh Street. Then, after Bobby talks to his folks, we might go and see a movie."

"Oh. Well . . . do you think that's . . . wise? I mean . . . don't you think Bobby's really tired? Because he's had such a long day, flying home from New York and everything?"

Weird question—and then I get it: Mom's afraid someone could be listening in. Which is a valid fear, I guess. And it certainly suits me, because now I can be vague. Which means I won't have to lie as much.

"Bobby says he feels fine. And we won't stay out real late or anything."

"But . . ."

And I know she's just dying to say, ". . . what about that man who talked to you at the library? What if he comes after you?"

She continues, "But you know I don't like you out after dark, Alicia."

"Mom—I *live* in the dark, remember? I'm okay,

really. And I've got Gertie here. Nobody messes with a German shepherd."

"Well . . . all right. But I want you home by ten-thirty, not a minute later."

And I say, "Mom, no. Eleven, okay?"

Because this is how we do our curfew dance.

And Mom says, "All right . . . eleven. Sharp."

Which is when she really wanted me home in the first place. But she always asks for an earlier time, and I always resist: push, pull, deal.

"Okay, Mom. Thanks. Talk to you later."

"Good-bye, dear."

There's a moment of polite silence in the car after I hang up, then Bobby says, "So let me guess—you don't have to be home until eleven, right?"

"That's what she said. But I can probably push it back again. The negotiation is never really over."

William says, "I hope you don't take this the wrong way, Alicia, that I'm making light of your . . . situation, or that I'm being too personal, but I must say, that was a *terribly* effective retort, about always living in the dark. I can't imagine a parent trying to reply to that line."

I nod. "It's one of my best. Along with, 'Try keeping your eyes shut for four years—then we'll talk.' "

"Brutal," he says. "Doesn't exactly make a person long for the joys of parenthood."

I hesitate, then, "I know this question is definitely too personal, but are you married?"

"Was," he says. "*Was* married. With a daughter. She's almost eleven now . . . no, make that twelve."

"So . . . you don't see her anymore?" I ask.

"It's been four years. Which is one of the things I plan to change, if we can—"

As the heavy car slopes around a corner, Bobby cuts into the conversation. "You know, William, if you'd talked like you were a human being instead of a monster when we first met in New York, things might have been a whole lot simpler than they are at the moment." Then he says, "Sorry. I shouldn't have said that."

A sober voice from the backseat: "No, I've had that coming. But honestly, Robert, do you think your father is going to be able to help me when he returns home from Europe on Sunday?"

That's my first clue about what Bobby said to make William so eager to hop into the backseat of a frozen car.

Bobby says, "I hope he can. Until then, we just have to keep you off of everyone's radar. Or sonar. Or infrared scanner. And . . . here we are."

The big station wagon slows, pulls sharply left, and as the nose of the car rises to cross the sidewalk into the driveway, the tailpipe scrapes the concrete behind us.

The car shudders to a stop, and Bobby says, "I'm parked here at the side kitchen door, sort of on an angle to block the line of sight from the street—can you picture that, Alicia?" I nod, and he says, "So, William,

Alicia and I are going to open both front doors of the car. I'll leave my car door open, open the door into the house, and then walk around to the passenger side to pretend like I'm helping Alicia. When I do that, you climb over the front seat and slip out the driver's side and into the house. And hold your breath—no vapor trails, remember? Here we go."

Twenty seconds later, both car doors have slammed, the door to the house is shut and locked behind us, and Gertie and I have been led up five steps from the landing into Bobby's kitchen. I hear Bobby flip a light switch, hear the hum of the refrigerator to my left, hear Gertie's claws on the tile floor.

Speaking softly, Bobby says, "Nicely done, everyone. William, you *are* here, right?"

"Yes," he whispers, "but I'm crouching, down below the level of the windows. All the shades are open, and your mentioning infrared scanners has made me altogether paranoid. Why is it so *cold* in here?"

I can feel Gertie move her head toward his voice, but calmly, so that's progress . . . I guess. I don't want her to get too comfortable around William. I'm beginning to trust him, I guess, but still, he's basically a stranger. A strange stranger.

Bobby says, "It's exactly sixty-two degrees in this house, which my dad thinks is an adequate evening temperature for sitting in a reading chair with a blanket, and according to him, it's also the ideal sleeping temperature. He's a global warming activist, and since he's the only one in the family who knows how to program the digital thermostat, my mom and I wear a lot of sweaters."

I hear Bobby cross in front of me, pull the refrigerator door open. And I imagine that I can feel more cold air spilling out into the chilly room. He shuts the fridge. Picks up where he left off with William.

"But the hot water heater in this house works great, never runs out. Back through the doorway we just came in? There's a stairway to the left that goes to the second floor. When you get to the hallway, the first door on the right is my room, the next one is the bathroom, then there's a guest room, also on the right. You can go up and take a shower, but don't turn on any lights. And I'll put a pair of my dad's pajamas in the guest room for you. And I think you should just get in bed and stay there— the less you move around, the better. For all we know, the FBI really might have heat scanners out there. Alicia and I are going to stay down here and try to look like we're just hanging out. I'll shut some curtains and blinds, but only a few—I don't want it to look like we're trying to hide anything. In case anyone's watching."

"The shower sounds wonderful, thanks. And I'll try not to slip and kill myself in the dark."

"I bet you'll do fine," I say, ". . . in the dark."

That gets a chuckle from William, and a few moments later I hear him creaking up the back stairs.

It's almost impossible to sneak around in one of these big old Victorian homes.

The shower starts running almost immediately, and Bobby says, "I've got to go out to the car for a second and get the box. I'll be right back. And then I've got to go up and air out the guest room, open all the windows. And I'm going to put an electric blanket on William's bed for him. Because I want him to have a really, really good rest tonight—know what I mean?"

I do.

I do know what Bobby means.

I hear him go down the steps and out the side door.

And I reach around until I find the breakfast table, and then a chair.

Because I need to sit down.

I need to take some deep breaths.

I need to stop feeling dizzy and scared.

I'm scared because Bobby mentioned the FBI again. And even though I know he talked about thermal scanners so William will feel like he has to get in bed and stay there, it's still true. A squad of agents really could be right outside, could come bursting in here any second.

And I'm scared because Bobby and I had only about five minutes of whispering back at my house, five minutes to plan out this whole evening. And that wasn't enough time, not really.

I mean, I think we thought of everything. And I love feeling like we're a team again.

But the truth is, it's impossible to think of everything.

So that means I thought of everything I could think of, and Bobby did his best too.

It's the things we *couldn't* think of.

Those are the ones that scare me the most.

chapter 17
blood on snow

I'm still sitting in the kitchen, and I've still got my coat on. Because William's right. It's freezing in Bobby's house.

I'd go upstairs and help, but I know Bobby doesn't need me right now. He's up there getting William's bed ready, and I'd just get in the way.

The bed.

William's got to stay in that bed, stay under that old electric blanket for most of the night—at least five hours, by Bobby's estimate. Because tonight the upstairs guest room is the laboratory. And William is our invisible mouse.

So I hope he's really tired—how could he *not* be tired? I know how burned-out I get, day in and day out. And I'm guessing that the last few days must have been a lot more stressful for William than they've been for me.

But that's just a guess. One more among so many.

One thing I know for sure—no way am I going to make it home by eleven. I need to stay here with Bobby, be ready to help. Just in case.

I dig in my pocket and get out my phone.

Because there are no guarantees here. If things go wrong, I need to be here . . . and there are so many things that could go wrong. I told Bobby I was in this all the way. So . . . really, I can't go home until morning.

Which means I need to stay right here. All night at Bobby's.

And his parents aren't home. And my parents know that.

And that's why I'm dialing Daddy's cell phone—instead of Mom's.

He picks up on the second ring, and I'm talking fast, before he can say a word.

"Hi, Daddy. I wanted to let you know that we're not going to a movie because Nancy called and asked me to come for a sleepover. So Bobby's taking me over to her house, okay?"

"Tonight? I don't think this is the best—"

"Really, it'll be fine, Daddy. Because there's no school tomorrow. It's a three-day weekend."

"Well . . . I guess . . . all right. But don't you to need to stop home first? Get your toothbrush and everything? And drop off Gertie?"

"I'll be fine, and Gertie's got some food I left there at Nancy's the last time."

"Okay then, but give us a call once you're there. And I know your mom'll want to talk to Mrs. Hamlin, all right?"

"Sure, no problem. G'night, Daddy."

"See you tomorrow, sweetheart."

And the phone gives me its little "call ended" handshake.

That was easy. Ridiculously easy. And Mom needing to talk with Mrs. Hamlin? I've got a way to deal with that.

The fake sleepover is a really old trick, a classic. I've never used it before, but some of my friends have.

But I'm not proud that it worked so easily. Because that just means my dad can't imagine me lying to him. And it's very sad that has to change.

Because sooner or later, reality *does* occur, and when it does, all the lies show up.

Like blood on snow.

Such a cheerful image. I'm not cut out for this secret-agent stuff. It's wearing me out, making me grim and morose. And also making me a liar.

I hear Bobby walking toward the kitchen from the front of the house, and when he's in the room, he says, "William asked if you'd come up there and talk to him a minute."

"Really? Why?"

"Don't know."

I say, "Should I go talk to him? I mean . . . should I?"

"Yeah, sure," Bobby says. "Can't hurt. But take Gertie with you, okay?"

I nod. "Absolutely." Then I say, "So . . . did *you* talk to him? Tell him what's going on or anything?"

"No—are you kidding? He shouldn't know anything about the process. Or at least nothing specific. And we don't want him to think that anything's supposed to happen tonight. He'd just get all tensed up. And, anyway, we don't know if this'll even work. That blanket has been stuffed in a box in a hot attic for two years. Wires get old and brittle, plus the controller got banged around by the U.S. Postal Service from Chicago to Florida and back. And when I checked the National Oceanic and Atmospheric Administration website, the geomagnetic storm activity is only about three-fourths as strong now as it was the last time this worked. There are so many variables."

Bobby's talking like his dad. Which he wouldn't like to hear me say. Bobby's about as fond of physics as I am.

I say, "Do you think he'll stay in the bed long enough? Like, what if he's the kind of person who sleeps for only a few hours? And what if he turns off the blanket?"

"That's not happening" and I hear a smile in Bobby's voice. "First of all, it's *really* cold in his room, and that electric blanket is the only cover other than the sheet. And when he saw it on the bed, he said, 'Fantastic! I *love* sleeping under an electric blanket.' But we already knew that, right?"

We did know that. Because sleeping under a particular kind of electric blanket that had a particular kind of malfunction when certain other conditions were just right—that's what triggered William's transformation, his disappearance. And the blanket on William's bed tonight is the exact blanket that caused the same phenomenon to happen to Bobby. And then the same blanket also caused Bobby's reversal. Because the identical stimulus seems to act like an on/off switch for the molecular modification.

Listen to me—it's Alicia Van Dorn, girl physicist. Daddy would be proud.

Bobby goes on, "And about William wandering around the house? I guarantee he's not leaving that room. I told him Gertie's going to be out in the hall all night. And I told him about her bad temper, and how she bit me on the ankle, even showed him the scars—which happen to be from a bicycle accident when I was fourteen. But he doesn't know that."

"You are *mean*, Bobby Phillips. Just plain *mean*. And devious too. Dangerously devious." I'm laughing, but it strikes me that it's true—the devious part. Because he just told another set of lies. We're both turning into world-class liars.

Bobby puts on a perfect British accent and says, "I'm only mean and devious when it's absolutely necessary, my dear. So it would be best if *you* stayed on my good side."

Then he's back to business, and the smile drains

from his voice. "Listen, I told him you'd be right up. The shades are down and the drapes are closed, so I told him he could use the little lamp by the bed, and he'll probably read awhile. But make it a short visit, okay? The sooner he calms down and dozes off, the better. I'll be in the TV room. My mom and dad are probably gonna call me in a few minutes."

"Oh," I say. "So they're really calling you?"

He says, "What—did you think I was making that up?"

I shrug. "It sounded fishy, that's all. Because they can call you anywhere on your cell phone, right?"

"Wrong," he says. "I've got the wrong kind of SIM card. So when they're in Europe, we have to use land lines—Little Miss Paranoid."

I ignore the jab and say, "Well, you have to admit that there are a *lot* of lies floating around. It's hard to keep track of what's true anymore." Then I give him a big smile. "And speaking of lies . . . remember Nancy's mom? You've met her, right?"

"Yeah . . . ," he says.

"Good, because I need your skills. You have to give a little performance later as Mrs. Evelyn Hamlin, talk to my mom and tell her it's all right that I'm having a sleepover at Nancy's house tonight."

"*Sheesh!*" he says. "And you're calling *me* devious? Like I said, I'll be in the TV room. And if you hear weird sounds floating through the floor, that'll be me, practicing my falsetto telephone voice. Now get up there and say nighty-night to William."

I salute. "Yes, sir."

Gertie's still in full harness, and when I stand up, she turns, comes up under my left hand, and presents the handle perfectly. "Good girl. Gertie, forward . . . good girl."

And we're through the kitchen doorway, then past the TV room, then walking straight through the living room toward the front stairs.

When we get to the tile floor in the foyer, I'll follow the wall around to the right, up the dark staircase, and then left to find the first doorway on the left—to pay a visit to the guest of honor.

And I'll talk to him a few minutes.

And I'm going to see if I can do that without telling any lies.

chapter 18
confessions

I knock on the door, and I'm sure he can hear the tentativeness in my little tapping. Because I don't feel good about this. Not at all.

"Come right in," he calls, and when I've got the door open, he adds, "but . . . could you leave your dog out in the hall? I don't think she likes me."

I smile at his concern, but there's no way I'm being in the same room with this man without Gertie. Real trust has to be earned.

"Don't worry," I say, "I'll hang on to her. And it's not personal—she's just confused about you, about the way you look."

"That makes two of us," he says.

I'm glad he's got a sense of humor. And I'm glad I've got one too. It's one of the things that's kept me sane these past three years. Or semi-sane.

I say, "So, Bobby said you wanted to talk to me?"

"Yes, if you don't mind," he says, and the mattress

creaks as he moves on the bed. "There's a chair about two feet to your left."

As he speaks, I form a mental picture of him sitting there with his back against the headboard, wearing a pajama top that's too big for him. And there are no hands coming out of the sleeves, and the neck hole is empty— or that's the way it looks. The way it would look. If I could see him—I mean, *not* see him.

I find the chair and sit. Bobby wasn't kidding. It's cold in here.

"Gertie, down . . . good girl." She drops to her stomach, but then inches forward at the bed until I tug on the harness. "Gertie, *stay* . . . good girl."

"Really," he says, "I just wanted to thank you again for letting me into your home earlier. You didn't have to do that. And I know it was a risk. So, thank you."

I nod. "You're welcome." Then I say, "Is there a light on? I mean, could you see me nod my head just then? Probably sounds like a stupid question."

"Not at all—and yes, there's a small reading lamp here beside me. The room's not bright, but I can see you. And the dog."

I don't know what to talk about, so I ask the first question that pops into my thoughts. "So what did you do in New York when it got this cold outside?"

"I stayed in hotels, mostly. Sometimes in a lobby, sometimes in an empty room. I'd follow a housekeeper into a room, stay out of the way until she was done cleaning, then lock myself in with the dead bolt. If a guest showed up later, their keys wouldn't work. And by the time the maintenance person showed up the next day to repair the lock, I'd be gone. I watched a lot of movies. And I started reading the Bible again—there's one in every room, you know. I also ate a lot of minibar snacks."

"Sounds sort of fun."

"Maybe for week or two. But I can tell you, it's no way to live. I eventually started squatting in an empty apartment. Still not much of a life, but it was sort of a reliable home base—until Robert spotted me."

I feel a current of anger there, and I want to keep away from anything that will upset him, so I keep the conversation moving. "And you stayed in New York for two years?"

"Two years, six months, and five days. Marooned on the island of Manhattan."

"But you could have gone anywhere, right? Why did you stay there?"

"I actually love the place. I'd been teaching at a university in Montreal, and I'd only been to New York twice before *this* happened. So I went, and I stayed. Best museums in the world—I love museums. And the plays, the Broadway shows, basketball games at Madison Square Garden, baseball at Yankee Stadium—endlessly interesting city, and all of it for free. If one must float about as a ghost, I can think of far worse places to be."

"Did you ever just want to walk into a hospital and ask for help? With the . . . condition?"

"Absolutely, but I always concluded that to be the focus of what would surely become a huge research project—that would be unendurable."

"And you didn't try to figure it out yourself? Because Bobby and his dad . . ." and I catch myself. Not supposed to talk about that.

But he sees where I was going, and says, "I was not so fortunate as to know a genius physicist in whom I could place complete trust. And I am not a math person or a science person. I am a words person, a literature professor. So the short answer is no, I had no idea about even where to begin to track down a cause."

"So you just kept going," I say, "one day at a time."

He doesn't answer right away. It's because of the way I said that.

Then, "Yes. I think you understand what that's like."

I say, "But at least I can hang out and talk to people. I'm kind of freaky, but I'm not, like, science-fiction freaky or anything. Didn't that kill you, not talking to people?"

"Oh, I talked to plenty of people. Especially priests. I used to go to St. Patrick's Cathedral almost every Saturday for confession. I'm not a Catholic, but I know how the system works. I'd wait around until there was no one in the queue, then I'd slip into a booth, pull the curtain, and whisper, 'Forgive me, Father, for I have sinned.' And then I could talk about anything. If I wanted to talk about a Knicks game, I'd say something like, 'When I was at the basketball game the other night and the Knicks were losing, I started wishing the Lakers guard would fall down and break his leg—was that a sin?' And then we'd have a good long talk about the game. New York priests love sports. I went to a lot of churches, all over the city, all kinds of churches. Slept in some too. I tried to go to a different church every Sunday. And I listened. But still, I listened by myself. I guess I'm just not cut out to spend this much time alone. I don't think anyone is. It's why people go crazy when they're in solitary confinement too long."

In the quiet room, a memory floods my thought. And I feel like it's okay to tell him about it. And I feel like it's my turn to talk.

"About three months after I lost my sight, my mom announced that we had to go and buy me some new clothes. I've always loved shopping for clothes, but the fact that I was never going to be able to pick out my own things again—it was like being stabbed in the heart. And I got angry, swearing and everything. But I went to Water Tower Place with her, and we went to this really nice store, a lot nicer than the places she buys her own clothes. But after about an hour I got fed up with my mom, fed up with the feeling of helplessness, and I refused to try on another thing. I snapped my white cane open and I tapped my way out of the store. Mom caught up and guided me to a bench, and she made me promise I'd stay put while she finished up in the store. And I did. And while I was sitting there, I heard someone come and sit down a foot or two away, on the same bench. And then there was a voice, a woman, and she said, 'I'm so glad to find you here today. I love talking to blind people. I go to the Chicago Lighthouse for the Blind once a month and I just talk and talk and talk. Nobody listens to me like blind people do—not even the priests.' That's exactly what she said. And in the years since then, I can't tell you how many strangers have come up and just started talking to me. It's like a free visit to a shrink. Or a priest. Because there's no risk. I'm not a threat. And I know that's why Bobby talked to me when we first met. A long time ago. And it's maybe why you talked to me in the library today. And why you came to my house."

And suddenly I'm embarrassed. I've said too much.

I've still got hold of Gertie's handle, and I can feel her sniffing, then pulling forward toward William's bed again. "Gertie, stay . . . good girl." And to get the focus off me, I say, "So what kind of sermons did you hear? When you visited all those churches."

"Pretty much the same thing everywhere. Be kind. Love your neighbor. Don't kill or lie or cheat or steal. And it's all true, and I think everyone knows that. It's the doing. The hard part is the doing."

A question forms in my mind, and I know I'm moving into dangerous territory here, but I ask it anyway. I have to. "Bobby told me that when he first met you, he thought you were a creep, sort of a psycho. How come? Because you don't seem that way at all to me."

He pauses, takes a deep breath, and lets it out slowly. When he talks, I hear such deep sadness.

"Thank you for that very great compliment. Most of what I said to Robert was made up, for effect. Fiction comes easily for me. I was trying to scare him into giving me information—a stupid ploy. But I did actually do some of the things I described to him, like spying on people. But only at the beginning. That's partly why I began going to those churches. I wanted to clean up my life, clean up my mind. I needed to reclaim my good name."

Gertie comes to her feet and pulls toward the bed, then yips a little. "Gertie, sit . . . *sit*! . . . Good girl." And I use her behavior as an excuse to stand up and move toward the door. Because this has already been much more of a talk than I'd thought it would be.

"I think my dog needs to go out now. It's been good to talk, William. And I hope things are going to work out for you." And quickly I add, "When Bobby's dad comes back."

"It's been good to speak with you as well, Alicia. And . . ." He waits a second, then two. "And I want you to know that my friends call me James. William is my middle name. I'm James William Townshend."

Another confession. And I know he's telling the truth. I can feel it in his voice.

I hope he can see my face from over here in the darkened doorway, get a glimpse of how glad I am to hear his real name.

Because I'm not going to say what I'm feeling. It would sound too personal, and it might make him uneasy to know that I'm getting so emotional about a stranger. Because right now, he doesn't seem like a stranger. More like a brother, someone I've known a long time. And I'm hoping with all my heart that he gets his second chance. I think he deserves it.

Because it's what we all need. We all need second chances, then third, fourth, on and on. All the fresh starts we can find.

I smile at him from the doorway and I say, "Thank you . . . James. It's nice to meet you."

chapter 19

still of the night

obby's dad and mom called while I was upstairs. They've changed their plans, and they're coming home Friday now. Not Sunday. Friday. That's tomorrow, arriving at three P.M.

And of course, Bobby didn't tell them about the houseguest, about William. I mean James.

Or about the FBI agents who've been following him.

Or about me staying here tonight. All night.

And about eight-thirty, when I call my mom, Bobby gives the performance of his life as Mrs. Hamlin, Nancy's mother. Best line: "Oh, yes, Alicia is *such* a dear. We just *love* having her come to visit us."

After all the phone calls, Bobby and I set up camp in the TV room. Tray tables, a couple of fleece blankets, some ice cream, some pretzels with this sweet mustard dip, and some root beer. All the essentials.

And for the past two hours it's just been couch time. We've had some small talk about music, and Bobby told me about some of his auditions, about how well he played, about some of the incredible musicians he met.

And I was tempted to ask him about Gwen, but I didn't.

I mean, I know Bobby would tell me everything there is to tell about her. But I don't want Gwen to be part of this night. Because we're balanced on this tiny pinpoint of time, just the two of us now. And before our parents reclaim us, before the man in the guest room wakes up, before some officer knocks on the door, we need to make the most of this night. This is our night. Ours.

So we've talked some about our parents, about things our families did during the summers when we were growing up. Sort of like stream-of-consciousness sharing, while Miles Davis and John Coltrane and Bill Evans spin out their sounds, one CD after another, all of Bobby's favorites.

This is good time. That's what I tell myself. And it is. It takes this kind of time for us to get to know each other, to get a feel for who that other person is.

But I keep thinking that this has to be our time to go deeper. Those tender feelings are in the air again, but down under so many other layers, pushed aside by so many other worries and concerns. Time bombs all around us.

Still, I keep hoping. Because Bobby and I and what we mean to each other—we're just as important as all this other stuff. And in the long run, I think we're *more* important. Much more important . . . aren't we?

During all this time, neither one of us has mentioned the man upstairs, William. I mean James.

I don't know what to do about that. I haven't told Bobby about the name. I feel like telling would be breaking a trust—because of the way he said it: "My friends call me James."

I don't think Bobby is his friend, not yet. Bobby doesn't want to be friends with him. Because when you're a friend, you care more, and more caring is always more risk. So Bobby won't let himself care yet. About William. About James.

That's what I tell myself. And I think it's true.

When it's ten-thirty or so, Bobby sneaks upstairs. He comes back two minutes later and says, "Lights out, and big snoring. The Phillips–Van Dorn Molecular Readjustment Facility is officially open for business."

He sits back down on the couch, closer this time. A big yawn.

"You getting tired?" he asks.

I nod, and answer with a yawn of my own. "Yeah," I say, "long day. A big day. Huge."

"Does Gertie need to go out again?" he asks.

"No, she's good. But is there another blanket, one she could lie on? It's a lot colder here than it is at our house at night."

"Sure," he says, standing up again, "and I'll grab another one for us. And a couple pillows."

Us.

He said *us*. Another blanket for *us*.

As in, another blanket for *us* to sleep under.

Us. Sleeping under a blanket.

And suddenly a voice rings out so clearly in my mind that I'm almost certain I'm really hearing it:

"Alicia? I need to speak with you."

It's Mom. The woman with boy radar.

But it's my imagination. She's not here.

And now I'm wishing the Brain Fairy would talk to me.

Hello? . . . Are you there?

Nothing. Never around when I actually need her.

I'm on my own here.

Pillows arrive. Another blanket arrives. For us.

And Bobby arrives. And here we are.

Us.

We're sitting up. And we're close. And we're sharing a blanket. And there's still music in the air, an all-night show on the radio, turned down really low. Subliminal jazz.

And I'm pretty sure all the lights are off now. Because I know that matters to most people. Me, I've always got the lights dimmed. I've got built-in ambience.

And now our heads are touching, sort of temple to temple.

He says, "So, did you miss me when I was away?" A trace of mint on his breath.

I nod, because he's that close.

Close enough to hear a nod. Breathing the same air.

All my hoping for a time when we could talk? Gone, vanished.

We both know there's been enough talking.

He changes position slightly. Almost face-to-face now.

And he reaches across under the blanket and rests his left hand on my side. Not high. Not low. Right on my ribs.

And his hand just stays there.

And I can feel the heat of his hand on my side, all the way through my sweater and all the way through my shirt. Resting there.

Or do I just imagine the heat?

Doesn't matter. I still feel it.

Gertie whines and gets up off the blanket on the floor, and in one fluid motion she jumps onto the couch beside me. And then she leans up against my back. Because she loves to be close.

And she leans right onto Bobby's hand. And he moves his hand, pulls his hand with all its heat back to his side of the universe.

And I think maybe Gertie has a deal with Mom, some kind of long-distance boy-patrol deal. Entirely possible.

Gertie jumps off the couch, curls up on the blanket again, and yawns, her mission accomplished.

But still, I can feel our moment coming.

Bobby's working up his courage, I know he is.

And I can wait for him, forever if I have to.

But I don't think it's going to take that long.

We've been this close before.

We've even kissed before—exactly one half time.

Because a fourth of a kiss plus a fourth of a kiss equals one half a kiss.

That's what we've had, two short, sweet, simple kisses. Shallow kisses.

Before.

Bobby stirs, moves closer again. And he buries one shoulder deep into the cushions of the couch. He moves, and I move too.

And we kiss.

We do. It is. I am. We are. Kissing.

No words.

Not needed.

Because I know. I'm not just his friend.

Something else now. Something more.

chapter 20
some friend

My left arm is killing me. And as the pain wakes me up, last night swirls into my head. I know where I am.

I'm on the couch. And this . . . this is Bobby. On top of my arm. And his breath against my neck.

And I'm back there, remembering last night.

Delicious.

I'm not moving. I don't care if my arm falls off. I am not moving. And I am mapping this moment, this scene, these smells, the sound of his breathing, the way Bobby and I are layered together on this couch, the way the hair on his arm feels under my fingers. Us. Sharing a blanket.

I free my right hand and slowly, slowly, I'm able to reach the watch on my left wrist. And I press the correct buttons, and it vibrates.

Six . . . nineteen.

So it's morning. Barely light outside.

My feet are freezing. And I reach down with one foot, feeling for Gertie on her blanket in front of the couch. Because she's always as close as possible. And she's always warm.

Not there.

And not on the couch to my right.

I snap my fingers, and I whisper, "Gertie, here." Because I would love a warm dog leaning against my back right now.

She doesn't come.

"Gertie, here!" I call.

No dog. And the grab of sudden panic.

I sit up and yank my hand from under Bobby's shoulder.

He says, "What?" all groggy with sleep.

And I shout, "Gertie? Gertie, *come*! Bobby—Bobby! Where's Gertie?"

And upstairs, I hear her.

She barks, twice. Then again.

She never barks.

Bobby sits up, then jumps to his feet.

"What's . . ." His voice is slurred, still in a dream. Then, awake, sharp, urgent. "Alicia, what's wrong?"

"Gertie, she's upstairs."

Bobby's gone, sprinting, and I hear him take the stairs on the run.

Gertie barks again, then her voice trails off into a garbled whine.

"Bobby—is she all right?" I'm screaming, terror now, on my feet. "Is she okay?" And I'm at the front staircase, running up the stairs, tripping, rushing ahead again.

I'm at the top of the stairs and Bobby calls, "She's all right, Alicia, she's all right—just a little wobbly."

I hear her whining, and I'm in front of her now, my arms around her neck, and there's sudden joy in her voice. And love, such love.

And tears spill out, the relief.

Then instantly, anger. The kind that strangles. "What happened, Bobby? Is she hurt—William! Did William hurt her? Because—"

He says, "No—actually, William gave her a treat. Some chunks of General Tso's chicken, looks like, with a couple of my mom's sleeping pills buried in each one."

"And he's—"

"Right," Bobby says. "Gone. And so is the blanket. And . . ." Bobby hangs the word in the air as his voice moves out the door and across the hall. "Yes. Also one of my dad's suits, plus some shoes, plus who knows what else. Gone."

"Did it work?" I ask. "The blanket, did it change him?"

Bobby says, "He took clothes, but I don't know. But taking the blanket, that has to mean something—maybe he took it to the FBI. Or to someone else. And if anyone was actually watching this house, either William slipped past them, or they were waiting for him. He's just . . . gone. That's all we know for sure."

"And that he poisoned my Gertie."

And I hate how angry I am, because this is the kind of rage that murder is made of. It's a good thing the man isn't here.

And I hear his voice, but now it seems twisted, mocking me: "My friends call me James."

Some friend.

Because a friend doesn't betray a trust, doesn't lie and steal and run away in the dead of night. And I'll never think of him as James, never again.

He's a creep, and his name is *William*.

chapter 21

n o w

I am not forgiving him. Those drugs could have killed Gertie.

It's Thursday again, so it's been a full week, and I can still feel the hot rage bubble up at the thought of his name.

William.

I am not forgiving him.

And I'm not forgiving myself either. To be so tricked, so totally bamboozled by that man's smarmy stories about solitude and church and all his *feelings*.

The Brain Fairy was right. Feelings are dangerous. So I'm trying to get my heart to be more obedient.

My heart.

That brings me to Bobby. And kissing.

Before the blindness, I know I saw thousands of kisses. I saw them with my own eyes. And in movies and on TV shows and up on theater stages, every kiss I saw had a sound, a shape, a motion—a beginning, a middle, and an end. Every kiss had its own little story line.

The kisses I saw in photographs and drawings, the ones in magazines and on book covers and billboards—those were the frozen kisses, just the middle bit, where the lips are touching, the arms are clinging.

The kisses in books, the ones described with words, those were the most powerful to me. Still, I soaked up the words so I could *see* the kisses.

So many kisses. I saw them with my own eyes, each one. I drank them in, photos, drawings, and words.

And all that seeing made me believe that I was preparing for kisses of my own. Seeing so many kisses made me think I was becoming an expert, that I'd know just what to expect, just how I'd feel when it was my turn to kiss. I thought I'd be ready.

I wasn't.

Because a real kiss, a kiss that two real people choose to give each other—it's something that can't be filmed or photographed or drawn, or even described with words. Because a kiss isn't what it looks like, or how it feels. A real kiss happens down deep inside of two hearts at the same time. It's hidden away. A real kiss is invisible.

And now I know what kissing is. So does Bobby.

But it's not like we've had any time to be together this week. Senior year is almost over, so schoolwork is intense for both of us, plus the college admissions process doesn't let up for a single day. And we're also staying apart in case there's still some trouble with the law, in case there's still surveillance.

Although, with each passing day, that seems more

and more unlikely. We haven't heard any more from the FBI, and no one in Bobby's family or mine has been able to spot anyone following or watching any of us. Which could mean they're not watching—or that they're really good at staying out of sight.

When Bobby's parents got home from Europe, his dad and my dad got together, but cautiously, and not at our house. And Daddy actually got one of those electronic sweepers so he could be sure there were no listening devices hidden in his study. Not that he and Dr. Phillips are planning to work on any more mice . . . or that's what they're telling us.

They're still preparing their data in case the secret gets out, preparing a fail-safe server upload, an emergency burst of information that would hit the Internet if it ever becomes necessary.

Because no one knows what happened to William. But if you ask me, he wouldn't have stolen that suit from Bobby's dad if he'd still been invisible. But I'm not going to think about him, because it just makes me upset. He's gone without a trace, so I say good riddance.

And if he stays gone, then I don't see how we could have any more problems with the FBI. No William, no evidence; no evidence, no case; no case, no FBI.

So for the moment, it looks like the secret remains a secret. And the two Science Dads actually made a solemn promise not to do any more research.

But they didn't promise to destroy the research

they've done. Because, and this is what Daddy said: "What if there's a security crisis, and it becomes clear that this technology *is* being used, that there are invisible agents out there doing evil things, hurting people? Or what if we discover that William took that blanket and sold it and everything he knows to some extremists? Then we'd have no alternative but to take everything we know and publish it, push it all out onto the Internet so everyone all over the world gets it at once. Because that's really all there is to our fail-safe plan. And we almost put it into action the day the FBI came to our house, the day I had to get rid of those mice. The message I left for Dr. Phillips at his hotel in Geneva that day—'our research has hit a snag'—the word *snag* was code, and it means, 'be ready to dump the contents of your laptop onto every server you can link to.' And if I'd told him 'our research has hit a brick wall,' then he would have published everything we know. If we ever do that, everyone would be able to understand the threat, everyone would know how to defend against it. And for all we know, there could already be dozens of other invisible people out there right now, being used, being exploited, doing really terrible things. If we ever discover that's true, we publish. And if we have to do that, there would certainly need to be more security measures worldwide. But once everyone knows, those measures would just be part of the routine, part of the new normal. Because if you *know* about this technology, it's not that hard to defend against it. And that will keep the playing field level. No awful surprises. At least that's our hope. Because sooner or later, this genie is getting out of its bottle. So we have to be ready, just in case."

About all the lying. Bobby and I are not lying at all, no more, either of us. Not to each other, not to our parents, not to anybody. And we told my mom and dad all about the fake sleepover gambit and all the rest of it, and explained why we had to do what we did. And we're sticking with the truth from now on.

Except I'm not sure about today.

Because Bobby's coming over to pick me up soon, and I don't know how he got out of school today, because this is Thursday. So I'm not asking him about that. Not today.

And even though this house is empty, we're not staying here together, because sooner or later Mom would ask me about that, and I'm not lying anymore.

So when he arrives, Bobby and Gertie and I are walking to the library, to room 307. Our study room. To do some studying. And some talking.

And this will be the first time we've been together in almost a week. I know Bobby's happy about it because he told me so. I've wanted to be close like this for so long. And now he wants that too.

Which is why I'm brushing my teeth one more time in the downstairs powder room.

And that's the doorbell.

Gertie's already at the door of the vestibule when I get there, and I open the heavy glass door, and she's at the wooden door now, and she's sniffing. And then she's growling and scratching.

And barking.

She never does that.

And I can't breathe, and my heart is up in my throat, and I want to rip the door open and let Gertie loose. I want to release the hounds. Because I know who's out there. And so does Gertie. She's barking and snapping and biting at the door, and I pull her back. "Gertie, hush . . . *hush*! Good girl," I say, because I don't want her to hurt herself.

I hear the latch of the storm door, hear it open, then the storm door closes, but not all the way. And above the pounding of my heart, I'm expecting to hear him speak. Because I know it's William out there.

Nothing.

Footsteps across the porch, down the steps. Then the gate squeaks, a door slams, a car drives away.

I reach up to the keypad and punch the alarm code. It takes me two tries because my hand is shaking so hard. "System is disarmed."

I turn the knob and pull, and there's something between the doors—leather. It's a briefcase.

I pull it inside, shut the wooden door, punch the keypad again. "System is armed."

In the family room I'm on the couch, and Gertie is leaning against my leg. She's still unsteady. Me too.

She sniffs at the briefcase, one of those big boxy ones, and she growls.

"I know, Gertie. I'm growling too."

I work the clasps, pull the flaps up, and open the top of the case wide. And I know what this is.

It's the blanket, folded up, with the wires and the controller in a neat bundle on one side. And on top of the blanket, a cassette tape. It's the old kind, pre-CD. I still use audiocassettes like this for some of the books I listen to, so I'm on my feet with the stereo cabinet open, pushing the right buttons. I put the cassette into the player.

William's voice.

More barking. "Gertie, hush . . . good girl."

I rewind and start the tape again.

"Alicia—first off, I am so very sorry that I had to treat your dog as I did, but I beg you to recall how extreme my situation was that day. Going into that evening, I did not know if I was being helped or if I was being set up to be turned over to the authorities. So I had to be ready for anything. Which is why I brought those chicken bits to Robert's house, just in case. By the time you and I had spoken, I felt quite sure I was going to be treated well, so I went off to sleep feeling silly to have thought ill of either you or Robert. About four in the morning, though, I awakened with a terrible pain in my head, drenched with sweat, and the electric blanket was crackling and popping. And for about five seconds it seemed like a bright blue light filled the room, and I thought I'd been blinded, or even electrocuted. I jumped from the bed and flipped on the light, and in the mirror atop the dresser, there I was. There I was! And it was at this moment that your dog came sniffing and growling at the door. I know how angry you must have been to discover that I used those pills to subdue her, and I'm very sorry about that. Again, please forgive my state of mind. Because the one line of defense I'd relied on for almost three years was gone, and there I was, fully visible, completely vulnerable. So I stuffed the chicken bits under the door, waited fifteen minutes, and then got myself dressed and out and away. Which leads us to now. In the smallest pocket of the briefcase you'll find some U.S. dollars, which should be enough to reimburse Robert's father for the clothing I took. My ex-wife has been an absolute brick, and she's sent me money and my passport and a plane ticket. And she and my daughter will be meeting me at the airport in Montreal this afternoon. I took the blanket, because it was obviously the thing that had caused my change, and I wasn't sure if the effect was permanent, or if perhaps a second treatment would be needed. And now I've brought it back to you because I'm sure you'll know what's best to do with it. I cannot ever thank you enough. Robert as well, of course. But if it hadn't been for your trusting me, I don't know what would have happened. And I'll never forget the kind things you said to me as I lay in that bed, in such deep despair. Again, my apologies, and my deepest thanks."

The tape hisses, and I reach up and push the stop button.

I guess I'm glad for William, but I'm not ready to forgive him for what he did to Gertie, and I am *not* going to let my feelings cloud my thinking. I'm *not*.

Because I *know* what I have to do. I'm going to get a pair of scissors from the kitchen, and cut this horrible blanket into bits, wad it all up and put it into a black plastic bag and walk it out to the curb and stuff it into one of our trash barrels. Because this is Thursday, and Thursday is trash day, and the big blue sanitation truck will be here soon. I want this whole thing out of my life forever, right now. Because I will *not* have this cropping up, bursting out like an insanity epidemic every couple of years. I *can't* have that. I *won't* have that. I want the future to be the way *I* want it to be, and I want all of this to leave me and Bobby alone, and I *don't* want—

Well, well, well, if it's not my overwrought little friend. Having a tantrum, are we? A wee bit of an existential hissy fit? Is that what I'm hearing?

No. NO. You are *not* invited to this. Just leave. I am working this out all on my own.

On your own? I've heard that one before. I've also heard the one about wadding up all the troubles and tossing them away. If only it were that simple. If only the big blue sanitation truck could pull up once a week and haul all the bad stuff away forever. So that the future would be all hunky-dory, all comfy-domfy, all cheery-deary.

Done yet?

No, I've still got to—

Because if you'll shut up now, I'll get back to planning my future. Because it's *my* future.

There! That's the problem, right there. Because you seem to think that there really is an actual future out there somewhere. And there's not. It's all now. *No future, no past, only now. Yes, you will get to another time, because that's what seems to keep happening. But when you get there, guess what? It's still going to be* now. *Forget about some perfect future. That's not happening. Work on now. Because* now *is all you're ever going to have.*

Are you done? Now?

Yes, I actually think I am. I think this may be the last time we ever talk like this. My work is done here. Now *it's up to you.*

Suits me fine.

I know. Otherwise I'd keep coming back.

So . . . no advice about what to do with the blanket, nothing more about Bobby and my heart, or how I ought to forgive William?

His name is James. Because you have to deal with things as they are, remember?

Of course I remember. Okay, his name is James.

Good. Alicia, it's been nice talking to you.

What . . . what did you just call me?

Alicia. That's who you are, right? At this mo-
ment? Right now? You're Alicia. Right?
Yes.
I thought so . . . Alicia.

I pop the cassette out of the tape player, and I put it back in the briefcase with the other stuff. And I close the clasps and I tuck the briefcase into the back of the closet over in the corner of the family room. Because I might get a call from Sheila one of these years.

But I don't have to think about any of this right now. I don't.

Right now, I'm going to go outside and start walking toward the library. Because I don't have to stay here at home, waiting for Bobby to come and get me. I'm pretty sure he'll be walking along Fifty-seventh Street, and then University Avenue until he gets to Fifty-fifth Street. So I'll start walking toward him. Might even meet him halfway.

And if we happen to miss each other, I'll just go to the library. To our study room. And he'll go there too. We'll find each other, I know we will. We always do.

"Gertie, come."

And we walk to the front hall together.

Hanger, table, bench, hook.

A place for everything, and everything in its place.

I open the closet, take my coat off the hanger, put it on, then shut the closet door. I pick up my scarf from the little table, wrap it once around my neck, and then

I button my coat, starting from the bottom and working upward. I pick up my hat, feel for the tag at the back, and then put it on my head, just so. I pick up my gloves, also on the table, and I put the right one in my right coat pocket, and the left one in my left coat pocket. I pick up my computer bag from the bench next to the table and put the strap over my right shoulder. I take the handle for Gertie's harness from its hook by the tall mirror. "Gertie, here . . . good girl." And I clip the handle on. Such a sweet creature. So patient. And loving.

And in front of the tall mirror, before I pull on my gloves, I stop and I reach out and I touch the silver glass. Cool and smooth.

And I stand here and I take a good long look at myself, right now.

And I like what I see.

It's me. I'm Alicia.